Fredd

The Journey
to Mei

Outskirts Press, Inc.
Denver, Colorado

The Journey to Mei
All Rights Reserved.
Copyright © 2007 Freddie Remza
V3.0

Outskirts Press, Inc.
http://www.outskirtspress.com

ISBN: 978-1-4327-0459-9

Library of Congress Control Number: 2007931096

Outskirts Press and the "OP" logo are trademarks belonging to Outskirts Press, Inc.

PRINTED IN THE UNITED STATES OF AMERICA

This book is dedicated to several people. To my husband, John, who lived through many months of revision. To my daughter, Chris, and granddaughters, Meghan and Brenna, who listened to the many stories of China. To my son, Eric, who taught me by example to go after something I wanted to accomplish. To the Stasko's, Carol and Mike, for their validation that what was written had merit. Last of all, to an amazing young American girl, Jenna, who just happened to be born in China.

Freddie Remza

Chapter Titles

Chapter One
Life Changing News

Being an only child is not necessarily a bad thing. I have my own room, my own stuff, and much attention. For ten years, my life has been just the way I wanted it—until today.

I needed a folder for a school project, and started rummaging through the desk in the front hallway. In the corner of my eye, I noticed a paper with my dad's handwriting. I picked it up and read it, but I didn't understand. I flew into the kitchen and found my parents sitting at the table drinking coffee.

"What's this?" I yelled waving the paper in the air. Neither of them said a word. They both sat there and stared at each other.

Dad put his cup down, smiled and said, "Shelly, we've been in touch with an agency over the possibility of getting a baby."

I felt the blood rush to my head as I heard him explain

there was a chance I'd be getting a sister—from China. They used the word adopt.

"What?" I asked. I sat down at the table and stared. Where is this conversation going? How do I make it stop?

"We've thought about this for some time," Dad continued, "and decided adoption is what we want to do."

"But why? What will I have in common with this little kid from China?" I cried out. I jumped up and accidentally knocked the chair over. Mom quietly picked it up and motioned for me to sit back down.

"This is not how we wanted you to find out, honey," Mom answered as she reached for my hand. I quickly pulled it away.

"I like being the only kid here. Why mess things up when they seem so perfect?"

"Shelly, you'll always be our daughter. We love you a lot. That's not going to change. But having a sister can be a wonderful thing. Aunt Carol and I enjoy getting together and talking on the phone. That's something you and a sister can have when you grow up."

"I have lots of friends. I don't need a sister."

"You do have friends. But a sister is different—it's family. Wouldn't you like to have a baby in the house? There's so much you can teach her."

"Mom, Dad! I don't get it. Why are you doing this?" I looked over and saw my dad smile.

"There's a need for families to come forward and adopt orphaned children who have few opportunities. We want to give one of these children a home."

I didn't know what to say. I knew I was being selfish, but that didn't change how I felt.

I turned around and stared out the kitchen window. I saw two squirrels run up and down the tall maples in my backyard. They distracted me for a few seconds, chasing each other limb to limb. I heard my parents' voices, but little came through to melt my stubbornness.

"Shelly, are you listening to us?" asked Dad.

"Yeah, but I can see there's no vote here."

"It'll be okay," Mom promised.

So many questions swarmed through my head; all I could manage was a sarcastic, "Sure."

I grabbed the folder that started all this and headed for my room, when a thought occurred to me. I twirled around and asked, "Where's this baby going to sleep? Not in my room."

"No, we plan on converting the office into a nursery," Dad answered.

"I'm glad to hear that."

"You know, Shelly, I'm going to need help decorating that room," Mom said. "What color scheme do you think we should use?"

I knew the motive behind this—to cheer me up. No way was that happening!

"Color scheme? That's easy. Purple, of course. That's my favorite color." For a brief moment, I felt victorious. She certainly won't go along with that suggestion.

"That's a great color. Purple it'll be."

"Humph," I grumbled, disappointed my suggestion didn't have the affect I had anticipated. "What's her name? The baby—does she have a name?"

"We don't have a particular child yet," answered Dad. "We still have to be approved."

"Approved?"

"Yeah, a social worker from the adoption agency will visit and check out our house."

"Why?"

"To make sure this is a good home."

"Will that adoption person be talking to me, too?"

"It's a possibility," answered Mom. "It takes about a year to get a baby once the papers are filled out. So if we're approved, we'll have plenty of time to choose a name."

"I don't know if I like this idea."

"Don't decide," advised Mom. "Maybe you should just agree having a baby in the house will be different, and different does not have to be a bad thing."

I returned to my room and threw myself on my bed. I stared at the ceiling and tried to figure things out. What will it be like having some other kid in the house? Exactly how will this baby change my life? Maybe it won't be so bad, I told myself. Many of my friends have brothers and sisters. They're all surviving.

Then there's my best friend, Amy. Her four year old sister, Gracie, is a real pain. She bangs on the door to get into Amy's room whenever we're in there sharing secrets. She barges in, sits down, and starts listening to our conversation. There's no privacy over there. But this new baby will be too small to do that, so that won't be a problem. At least not right away.

I returned downstairs and found my mom stacking the dishes in the dishwasher.

"Is it okay if I tell someone, like Amy, about this?"

"I don't see why not. Sure, go ahead."

I picked up the phone to call, but then remembered she was at her grandmother's house for Sunday dinner.

"Great! Now I'll have to wait until I see her on the bus tomorrow," I mumbled under my breath as I climbed the stairs leading back to my room.

Amy's been my best friend since first grade. We've done everything together. If I'm not at her house, she's at mine. Both of our moms tell us we're like "two peas in a pod," but I have absolutely no idea what that means.

I flung my body back onto the bed, but this time landed

on something bumpy. It was Miguel, my stuffed armadillo. I've had him since I was seven. Most kids like bears. Me? I like armadillos. They have the right idea. If something threatens them, they roll up in a ball and hide. I wish I could do that.

"Miguel, why do I feel threatened by this new kid? What am I afraid of?" I picked Miguel up, hugged him to my chest, and thought about tomorrow.

Chapter Two
Sharing the News

The big yellow bus approached Amy's stop and she got on. I immediately began to fill her in.

"Adopt? From China? That is sooo amazing! You are sooo lucky!"

"I am? But you're always complaining about Gracie? You're forever griping about how annoying she is!"

"Oh, HER. Yeah, you're right about that! But this is different, Shelly. This will be a cute baby; not an obnoxious sister."

Her unexpected response confused me. I said nothing but stared out the window.

"Is the baby in China now?" Amy asked breaking the silence.

"We don't have a baby picked out. She might not even be born yet."

"So how do you know it'll be a girl?" Amy asked.

"My mom said most of the babies in the Chinese

orphanages are girls."

"Why's that?"

"I don't know, Amy. Anyways, we still have to be approved by the adoption agency."

"And then what?"

"Then we wait for a referral," I said.

"What's a referral?" she asked.

"It's some kind of a letter about the baby they've matched us up with," I explained. "My parents said it takes a long time before we get this referral."

"How long?" Amy asked. The bus came to a complete stop as it picked up the last load of kids.

"Probably around a year."

"A year? That's a long time to wait."

"I know. But it'll go by fast. That kid will be here before you know it." I started gathering my things together as the bus turned onto Cherry Street.

"How does she get here, ya know, from China?" asked Amy.

"We fly over to pick her up."

"Fly to China? Wow! Will your parents be taking you, too?"

"Yeah, they want me to go. They think seeing China will be a good experience for me. My dad said it's important for us to know about the country she comes from—their traditions and stuff."

"China! That's so far away."

"Yup, it's on the other side of the world. Oh, guess what? My mom said I could help decorate the nursery. She's letting me choose the color. What do you think about purple?"

"Purple? That's neat! It seems like all baby girls have pink; purple will be different."

Amy's enthusiasm over this news of mine started to rub

off on me. Not much; just a little. Who knows? Maybe this won't be so bad. Then again, it could be a disaster.

The bus pulled up in front of Madison Elementary. I dragged my backpack behind me as I stepped off the bus. I looked up and for the first time noticed the trees on the hillside starting to transform into their reds and yellows. "Autumn is here," I mumbled to myself as I buttoned up my sweater to keep away the morning chill.

The halls were unusually crowded and noisy as Amy and I made our way to the intermediate wing. Mrs. Standish, my fifth grade teacher, stood at the classroom door smiling and greeting everyone as she's done every morning. I liked my teacher. She had this pleasant way of making us feel important to the room. Everyone needs that once in awhile. Even me—especially today.

"Good morning, girls!"

"Good morning, Mrs. Standish."

"Did you ladies have a good weekend?"

"Yeah," Amy quickly responded. "Guess what, Mrs. Standish? Shelly has some exciting news to tell you!"

"Really? What is it, Shelly?"

"Oh... Well, I guess I'll be getting a sister soon. My mom said she'll be coming from China." There must have been a weird look on my face because Mrs. Standish waited a few seconds before she answered.

"Wow! That is exciting news. So how do you feel about it, Shelly?" Mrs. Standish always knew what to say.

"I don't know. Sometimes I think it'll be okay to have a sister and someone else at my house. Other times I like things the way they are, and really don't care to change anything."

"Oh, I think that's perfectly normal. I bet you'll be more excited after all this settles in. Besides, look at the fun you'll have getting ready for her arrival."

"Yeah, I guess." I looked down at the floor tiles and saw the scuff marks that were put there by the many sneakers passing through the hallway everyday.

"Would it be okay with you and your parents if I mention the adoption to the class?"

"Sure," I said. "That's alright."

"Good. Well, girls, why don't you go into the room and get yourselves organized for the day. And, Shelly, thanks for sharing your news with me."

Chapter Three
A Geography Lesson

As soon as I walked into the room, I got ready for the morning ahead. I didn't feel like talking to anyone. Mrs. Standish took the attendance and lunch count. We stood for the Pledge of Allegiance as it was broadcasted over the loudspeaker, and then everyone sat down at their desks. It was the beginning of a normal school day until Mrs. Standish suddenly pulled down the map of the world.

"Class, we usually have math at the start of each morning, but today I have something else to talk about." She brought up the Pledge to the Flag, and how we say it to show respect to this great country we all live in.

"America was formed by many people from many countries. Some immigrated as adults. Some came as families. And more recently, some arrived as adopted children."

I immediately sat up straight when I heard her say that.

Mrs. Standish continued, "Shelly just told me her

family may be adopting a baby from China." Everyone in the room turned around and smiled at me. The same questions Amy asked on the bus were on their minds, too.

After everyone quieted down, Mrs. Standish pointed to China on the map.

"China is a very large country. It's also a very old country. If we were to think about countries as we do people, the U.S. would be a newborn baby, while China would be an elderly person. The Chinese don't think about their history in the hundreds of years like we do in America. Their history is in the thousands."

"Thousands of years?" Jeffrey blurted out. "That's before the knights and King Arthur!"

Jeffrey always talked about medieval times. Whenever our class went to the library, he'd sign out books on lords, castles, and Robin Hood. His brain was just plain stuck there.

"You're right," Mrs. Standish said patiently. "In fact, a Chinese civilization existed thousands of years before the Medieval Ages."

"I heard on the History channel that the Chinese invented paper," said Rachel.

"They did. As a matter of fact, they're one of the oldest known civilizations on Earth."

Mrs. Standish explained how living in China was not at all like living in the United States.

"Life is quite different over there. While the people in China do not have as many things as us, they still manage to take care of each other. Most people live in crowded apartments. In some places they don't even have running water. Even in the large cities, people either drink bottled water or boil the water they use from the tap."

Crowded apartments? No running water in some places? I was surprised not everyone had running water.

"You know, kids, today many Chinese people are moving from the country to the city. Slowly they're changing their ways. Still, tradition is very important. People do things in much the same way as they've done for hundreds of years. Grown children often live with their elderly parents. They grow up knowing they'll help each other out. They're good people."

After our lesson on China, Mrs. Standish asked us to take out our math books. As I tried to locate my homework paper, she walked over to me and whispered, "Shelly, sometime next spring I'll be assigning a research project. When that time comes, consider doing it on China."

I nodded my head and said, "Sure."

Everyone in the room was into the lesson on triple digit multiplication, but I wasn't. I kept thinking about what Mrs. Standish had said a few minutes earlier. Families live with each other and take care of each other. If that's the case, why are there so many children in orphanages waiting to be adopted? Where are their parents? Why aren't THEY taking care of them? All these questions bothered me. I'll ask Mom. She'll know.

Chapter Four
Getting Some Answers

After hearing Mrs. Standish talk about China, I wanted to know more. Actually, I needed to know more. Unlike other school days, this one moved forward in slow motion. Eventually 3:30 showed itself on the clock, and the dismissal bell sounded. I was finally on the bus going home.

I ran into the house looking for my mom. She was always there since she didn't have a job like Amy's mother. After a little searching, I found her in the laundry room folding towels.

"Mom, I told Mrs. Standish we're adopting a baby."

"Oh? What did she say?"

"She thought that was a good thing. She also gave my class a little lesson on China."

"That was nice of her," Mom answered as she took a towel from the basket.

"I'm confused about something she said."

"What's that?"

"She said families in China take care of each other. If that's true, why are there so many children in orphanages waiting to be adopted?"

"Yeah. Well, that's a hard question to answer. Here, Shelly, help me with these towels and I'll try to explain."

I reached for one of the towels and stretched it out on the table. I looked over at my mom. I saw her raise her eyebrows and twist her mouth. It was a weird look, but always a look she gave whenever she was thinking about what she would say.

"Before I answer your question, Shelly, I need to tell you what happened in 1979."

Mom explained how the Chinese government made a new law. It had to do with the huge numbers of people living in the country.

"There was a population explosion in China. Families were having too many children. The government worried there could be serious problems in their country if this continued," she said.

"What kind of problems?" I asked.

"Not having enough places for everyone to live, for one. As it is, many large families, especially in the city, live in one bedroom apartments."

"Only one bedroom?" I asked thinking about how I have one bedroom all to myself.

"Only one," answered Mom. "But that's not all. If the birth rate didn't slow down, there wouldn't be enough food or jobs for everyone. So a law was passed telling parents they could only have one child."

"How did the government make the people do that?" I asked as I put my pile of folded towels in the laundry basket.

"At first they didn't enforce the law. But then in the

1990's they became very strict. The people who followed the 'one child rule' would be given many privileges and rewards."

"Did the people like this new law?"

"Let's say it was especially difficult for those who lived in the country. They were against it because they needed a large family to help with farming chores. So the government told them if they lived in the country, they could have two children."

"In school I learned when America was settled, there were large families for that same reason."

"That's right," Mom answered. "As for China, the Chinese people seemed to accept the 'one child law' in the city because they didn't have enough living space. Apartments were already small and very crowded."

I followed Mom into the living room. She sat down on the couch and motioned for me to sit next to her.

"I bought this picture book on China. I thought maybe you'd like to look at it. It has some interesting photos in it."

"Mrs. Standish told me she'll be assigning a research paper in the spring. She thought I should do it on China. Do you think I could use this book?"

"Sure! Whatever you learn about China, you can teach Dad and me."

I opened the book but then remembered the questions I had on my mind. "Mom, I still don't get why there are so many kids in the orphanages, and why most of them are girls."

"Boy, you're sure good at hard questions. Let me start by explaining one of their customs. When people get old, it's expected the parents will live with their son and he'll take care of them. If they have a daughter, she'll live with her husband's family and help take care of his parents. So if they don't have much money, it's very important for them to have a son."

"What does that have to do with the orphanages?" I asked as I laid the book of China down on the coffee table.

"Remember, they can only have one child. If that one child ends up being a daughter, they worry no one will be there to take care of them in their old age."

"So what do they do?" I persisted.

Mom sighed, "Well, the way I see it, they have three choices. First, they could choose to have the one daughter. This would be fine if they had enough money to take care of themselves in their older years. But what if they didn't?

Another choice would be to break the law, pay a huge tax, and hope the next baby is a boy. Again, there's the problem of no money to pay the penalty tax."

"What's the third choice?" I asked.

"The third choice would be to secretly give up the daughter, try for another child, and hope it's a boy."

I sat there thinking about what she said. I understood Mom's words, but had trouble accepting what they meant. I finally asked, "If they had a girl, would they take her to an orphanage?"

"Orphanages do not accept babies who have parents. So the mother would have to leave her baby at the door of an orphanage or some other public place where she's certain the child would be found."

"She'd just leave the baby?" I asked.

"If they're poor and can't afford the large tax for having two children, she might think there's no other choice."

"Would you do that, Mom? You know, leave a baby?"

"I'd like to think I wouldn't, but no one really knows what they'd do if they're caught in a hopeless situation."

"That's so sad."

"It is sad, but I think it's also important for a baby to know her birth mother did not leave her because she wasn't loved. I've heard when a baby is left to be found; somewhere hiding in the shadows is a parent watching with tears in her eyes. Sometimes a note is attached asking someone to take care of the baby as she was unable to."

"Does that happen a lot?"

"It does. But remember, that's not what we think should happen. Certainly that's not what all Chinese people do. But there are many who are poor and have absolutely no help. They might decide they can't take care of the baby; that the child would be better off adopted by people who can offer her a better life."

Reaching over to the coffee table, I picked up the book and looked at a colorful picture of a city. It showed many tall modern skyscrapers amongst a sea of people.

"China doesn't look like it's poor," I pointed out.

"China is a huge country," Mom said. "Did you know it's larger than the United States? Because of its size, there are lots of differences from one part of the country to the other. That picture is of Shanghai which is a large business center in China. In the picture you..."

I could hear Mom talking about Shanghai but I couldn't concentrate on her words. Instead I focused on what she told me earlier about the babies, the orphanages, the problems of the people living there.

"Mom, do you think that's what happened to the baby we'll get, you know, get dropped off?"

"It's possible, Shelly. Most of the children who are in orphanages are little girls. I'm sure her mother was very upset when she gave her up. They love their babies, but if they had more than one child they would have to pay that huge fine. Remember, this amount was more than they could ever make at a job. It's a big problem for them."

Mom went on to tell me how some children may also have health problems when they're born. If their parents

don't have the money to pay for medical treatments, they
might give the child up for adoption hoping someone
would provide the help the child needs.

"I guess I thought anybody who is sick would be
helped."

"If we need medical assistance in the United States, we
have ways to get that help. That's not always the situation
in other countries of the world," Mom said.

"I feel kinda bad about all this."

"I know. Some things are hard to understand. But China
started allowing people outside its country to adopt these
babies. They wanted to make sure these children had a
good life, wherever that may be."

Both of us sat there without saying a word. Sometimes
that's the only thing you can do. After a few minutes had
passed, my mom asked, "Do you have anything more you
want to ask me?"

"No, not now."

"Are you sure?" questioned Mom.

"I just need to think about all this, that's all."

"I know. There's a lot to think about. Well, I'm going
to get dinner started. If you have anymore questions, just
ask. Okay?"

"I will."

After I watched Mom leave the room, I went upstairs
to my bedroom and stared out the window. I saw our
green van parked in the driveway. It wasn't a brand new
car, but it ran well. I saw Josh, who lived across the street,
ride the new bike he got for his birthday last month. I
turned away from the window and noticed the books, toys,
and clothes I had in my closet and on my shelves. I opened
the door to the hallway and walked over to the room that
would one day be the nursery. It was empty with only the
computer, a file cabinet, and a large desk chair occupying

its space.

I thought about the children in the crowded orphanages. I imagined the babies, sometimes two in a crib, all alone without a family. Who will hold them or play with them?

Mom told me there were nurses, but they're in charge of so many children. Those babies don't have a family like I do. I knew what needed to be done. I rushed downstairs and found my mom in the kitchen.

I walked up to her and announced, "It's good we're adopting this baby. She'll need a family and I'll be happy to share mine with her."

Mom came over and gave me a hug. She smiled and said, "We have enough love in this family to include one more person, don't you think?"

I nodded my head, and for the first time, I knew in my mind and in my heart I wanted to be a sister. There was no longer any doubt. Yes, it'll be good. Matter of fact, having this baby from China will be very good. Good for the baby, good for my parents, and even good for me.

Chapter Five
The Home Visit

A month had gone by. My parents were busy meeting with people at the adoption agency, filling out papers, and making phone calls. Every time something was completed, Dad would say, "We can check that off our list."

My parents had to answer a lot of questions. They gave the adoption agency names of people they could contact to find out more about us.

"These names are our references," Mom explained. "See? Amy's parents are listed."

"Why does the adoption agency do this?"

"To make sure we're the right family for this baby."

We met Mrs. Dillon, a social worker, and arranged for her to come to our house for a required home visit. Mom cleaned the house from top to bottom, and then cleaned it again. Dad fixed everything that needed to be fixed for the past two years. At least that's what I heard my mom tell

Mrs. Baker, our next door neighbor. And me? I picked up my room to "make it look presentable". Those were the exact words Mom used whenever she wanted me to clean it.

The doorbell rang and I peeked out the window.

"It's Mrs. Dillon," I announced to my parents.

"She's right on time," my dad pointed out as he walked over to the door.

"Hello, Stacy. Come on in."

"Hi, Steve, what a nice place you have here."

"Thanks, we've lived here for almost twelve years. It's such a friendly neighborhood."

I noticed Mrs. Dillon mentally writing everything down in her head.

"Can I get you some coffee, Stacy?" Mom asked.

"Thanks, Kathy. I would love a cup. It's been a long day."

After Mom left the room to get the coffee, Mrs. Dillon pulled her pen and clipboard out from her briefcase.

"The BCIS requires me to ask you all these questions," she said to my dad.

"What's BCIS?" I asked.

"Oops! Thanks for asking. I sometimes forget not everyone knows what those letters mean. BCIS stands for the Bureau of Citizen and Immigration Services."

"Oh," I nodded, not really understanding all of that. Guess it must have something to do with adopting a baby from another country.

After Mom entered the room with the coffee, Mrs. Dillon said, "One thing you'll need to do is child proof your house. Make sure all medicines are locked up; no loose cords on the window blinds; and all unused electrical sockets covered up."

Dad nodded in agreement. "We'll take care of all that."

"That's good. How about guns, Steve? Do you have any in the house?"

"No, we don't own a gun."

"Then I don't need to ask how they're stored," she smiled as she checked off another item.

"This house doesn't look that old, so I'm guessing the electrical and plumbing are all okay?"

This time both my parents nodded their heads.

"Before I leave, could I see where the child's bedroom will be?"

"Sure, we can show you," Mom answered as she jumped from her chair. "The nursery isn't completed yet. Right now we use the room as a home office, but we plan to move the desk and computer out."

"That's fine. I just need to see the room." We all stood and went upstairs. Mrs. Dillon walked in, looked around, and said, "This looks very nice. It's certainly a good size."

"Guess what? I'm going to help decorate it," I proudly told her.

"That'll be a wonderful project for you. Decorating can be such fun. By the way, where's your room, Shelly?"

"Down the hall. You wanna see it?"

"Sure."

"I spent yesterday cleaning it up and making it look presentable." Everyone laughed. I had no idea why that was funny. Grownups can be weird at times.

"Looks like you did a great job," Mrs. Dillon said as she glanced into my room. "It's very presentable."

As we headed downstairs, she asked, "What kind of crib will you be using, Steve?"

"Crib?" asked Dad. "It'll be the same one Shelly used when she was a baby. Why?"

"Just wondering if its slats are far apart? If they are, then the baby's head could get caught in between."

"Oh, no! The crib's only ten years old."

"That should be fine," said Mrs. Dillon.

After a few more questions, Mrs. Dillon announced, "I'll be filing my report with the BCIS and the CCAA. I don't expect there to be any problems. Everything looks good."

Mrs. Dillon looked over at me. "Are you wondering what CCAA stands for?" she asked as she put her papers away in her briefcase."

"Yeah."

"I knew it! It stands for Chinese Center for Adoption Affairs. Can you remember all that?"

"I don't know. Will I need to?" Everyone started laughing again.

"So what's the next step?" Dad asked Mrs. Dillon.

"Well, let's see, you've been fingerprinted. You submitted proof of citizenship along with your marriage certificate, and we received your medical forms. When the time gets closer, you'll need a visa. Do you have a passport?"

"We applied for one last week," Mom answered.

"Did you send in your income tax records yet?"

"That's already been done," my dad said.

"I think all that's needed is my home study report. I'll be mailing you a copy before I send it in. When you receive it, check it over to make sure all of the information is correct. Meanwhile, use this time to get things ready for the baby just like you did when you were waiting for Shelly to be born." Mrs. Dillon looked over at me and winked.

"Does everything go to Beijing?" my mom asked.

"Yes, all of your papers will be placed in what is called a dossier. They're checked and registered there."

Mom asked, "What happens to the dossier once it's there?"

"It'll be matched with a child who's available for adoption. Each child also has a dossier that the orphanages from the different provinces of China put together."

"What's in this dossier?" asked Dad.

"The child's photo, some observations of her, and a medical report," said Mrs. Dillon.

"Do these go to the CCAA?"

"Yes, when the child is matched up with a family, it's called a referral."

"I heard this referral can take as long as a year," Mom told Mrs. Dillon.

"It could. When the adoption agency receives it, they'll give you a call. You'll meet with them and decide if you want the child that's being offered. If you decide you do, there's usually a wait of several weeks before you receive a document giving you permission to travel. Once you get that, you hop on the plane!"

Mrs. Dillon stood up to leave. "Thank you Steve, Kathy, and Shelly for this nice visit. So, Shelly, what do you think about all this?"

"Everything seems so complicated. My brain is filled with confusing words like dosey something, CCAA, documents, Bureau of Citizenship ahhh, whatever it is."

Mrs. Dillon grinned. "I think you mean dossier and Bureau of Citizenship and Immigration Services!"

After she left, we stood by the door and watched her drive off. Then Dad headed over to the closet and took out his coat. "Well, I'm glad this home visit thing is over. Shelly, you were great. Tell you what! I'm hungry. Let's go grab a pizza."

"Sounds good to me!" I said.

Chapter Six
Lots to Do and Christmas, Too!

December made its appearance last week with temperatures around 30 degrees. Yesterday we had our first snow day, and the girls on my street used our day off from school to build snowmen, make snow angels, and dodge snowballs that the boys threw directly at us.

The sights and sounds of the holidays were everywhere. Men and women, wrapped up in coats and scarves, stood at their posts ringing bells as people passing by threw stray coins into their red kettles. Everyone was busy getting ready for the 25th. A few days ago, Dad and I went Christmas shopping to buy my mom a present. I found a red plaid scarf that would be a perfect replacement for her old one with frayed edges.

At school, the fourth and fifth grade chorus had their concert last Tuesday. We performed for the teachers and the kids in the afternoon. In the evening we had a second performance for our parents. I love this time of year. I think most kids do.

"Mom, did you know Amy doesn't celebrate Christmas?"

"Yes, I did. Her family is Jewish so they celebrate Hanukkah instead."

"Yeah, instead of a Christmas tree in their house, they have a menorah that holds nine candles. For eight nights, they have a special meal when one of the candles are lit. Then everyone exchanges a gift."

"Now that's a good way to do it," Mom said. "This way you enjoy each gift as you receive it instead of opening them all at once."

"You know what I want for Christmas?"

"A new video game," Mom answered.

"Well, er, yeah, that sounds good. But what I really want is my new sister!"

"Is this from the girl who didn't want anyone sharing her space?" Mom teased.

"I know. I've changed my mind."

"I'm glad you're okay with all of this now, Shelly. It makes things so much easier."

"When do you think we'll be getting the referral? I have my fingers crossed it'll be soon."

"I'm afraid we have another eight or nine months to wait."

"Waiting for the referral is like waiting for Christmas," I pointed out.

"We can use this time to get ready for the baby as well as for Christmas. We have all the official stuff done. All we can do now is get the house ready."

"Mom, I'm glad China lets us adopt."

"They didn't always. It didn't start until around 1992

when the Chinese government passed a law saying that children from their country could be adopted by people from other countries."

"Is that when they came up with all of those rules we had to pass?"

"You bet."

"Waiting is sure hard," I said as I turned the TV on.

My parents spent several weekends changing the computer room into a purple nursery. Dad painted the room a pretty plum color. It made the walls pop out. Then he dragged my old crib down from the attic. He set it up and my mom bought brand new sheets and blankets.

I turned from the TV and said, "I love the small purple balloons that are at the bottom of the baby's quilt."

"I was lucky finding that quilt. Did you see what I did with that old changing table?"

"No."

"Come, look and see."

We went upstairs to the nursery and there stood the table Mom found at the used furniture store.

"It doesn't look shabby or smell musty anymore!" I yelled out in surprise. "How did you get it to look so good?"

"I gave it a good scrubbing with bleach and painted it white."

"It's like new."

"Look, I washed all of these baby clothes. Would you like to fold them and put them in the dresser?"

"Okay. I like doing stuff like that."

Mom handed over the laundry basket of clothes. "The problem is we have no idea when the baby will be coming. We have to be ready at a month's notice. So we'll take care of what we can right now, and then we won't be rushed."

"Mom, won't these clothes be too small for her? They say six months."

"No, even though the baby will probably be around ten months old by the time we get her; she'll most likely be wearing clothes that are for a six month old child."

"Why's that?"

"It's because the children are in cribs for most of the day. That can interfere with their growth. I heard a good way to figure out their size is to subtract one month of growth for every three months they're in the orphanage."

"I see." I turned around and noticed a roll of wallpaper trim sitting on a table. "Where did you find this?"

"That's my biggest discovery," said Mom. "Check it out! It has the same purple balloons that are on the quilt."

"Everything matches," I said looking from the wallpaper to the quilt.

Mom shook her head and said, "I thought that was a great idea of yours—stenciling two balloons on one of the walls."

I walked over and touched the balloons that appeared to be drifting to the ceiling. "I finally got the courage to draw it on the wall after practicing it on scrap paper."

Mom took another look at my art work. "It turned out nice."

We walked back into the living room and stopped to admire the Christmas tree that we decorated the night before.

"You know," Mom said, "next Christmas will be so different. This will be the last one with just the three of us."

I took two of the ornaments off one branch and rearranged them on another. "I have an idea! Can we find a tree decoration that has something to do with China?"

"Yeah, we can look for one the next time we're out shopping," said Mom.

Just then we heard laughter and rustling noises coming from outside. The doorbell rang and I ran to open it.

Standing in front of our door was a group of people in coats, scarves, mittens, and boots. I didn't have to wait too long to find out why they were at our house. They were Christmas carolers who, on cue, sang "Silent Night."

Dad came into the room to see what was going on. "It's a good thing they're dressed for the weather. The snow's coming down."

I looked past the bright flood lights that beamed onto the decorated wreath hanging on our front door. I saw large white flakes sticking all over their clothing. Their smiles, swaying bodies, and enthusiastic gestures brightened the dark night as their voices harmonized into a second verse. When they finished, Mom offered the group Christmas cookies. They eagerly grabbed them from the plate and scooted off to the next house singing, "We Wish You a Merry Christmas."

Chapter Seven
The Shower

"SURPRISE!"

"What's going on?" my mom squealed. "Carol, Mom! Why's everyone here?"

"We're giving you a surprise baby shower," Mrs. Baker explained as she pulled my mom over to a special chair in the center of the room.

"I thought I was coming over for lunch," Mom told the group of family and friends. She looked over and saw me. "Shelly, you knew about this?"

I laughed and said, "Everyone knew about it."

"This was such a well kept secret," Mom said. I don't know what to say. What a surprise!"

Not only were many of our friends and neighbors there, but Mrs. Baker invited my grandmother, Aunt Carol, and my cousin, Stephanie. My mom and Mrs. Baker were friends since before I was born. They do a lot together, and it's not unusual for my mom to run next door or for Mrs.

Baker to be over at our house.

I had never been to a baby shower. When I walked in I noticed decorations scattered around the room. I saw a stork with a funny accordion body standing at the edge of the food table. At another table there stood a huge baby bottle filled with all sorts of things—lotion, baby shampoo, powder, diaper pins, bibs. Everyone at the shower put something into that bottle.

"Look at the pink hearts," Stephanie said.

Mrs. Baker explained, "Do you like those? I thought with Valentine's Day around the corner, hearts would be a fitting theme for the shower. Besides, they were so easy to find."

I was excited to see Stephanie at the party. It gave me someone to hang out with. Grownups can be so boring at times. Stephanie was eleven and in sixth grade. Even though she's a year older than me, I'm taller. Our relatives tell us we look alike. We have the same kind of face, but I have brown hair while her hair is red. She also has braces on her teeth. I'm happy I don't need them.

Whenever I go to my grandmother's house for a fun sleepover, she has Stephanie over, too. At bedtime, one of us gets the giggles. It never fails. Before long, Grandma's in the room with the "you better go to sleep" warning. I'm lucky I have her for a cousin. She makes me laugh.

Stephanie and I were first in line at the buffet table. "Looks like the first thing ya do at a shower is eat," she snickered.

"I'm all for that. I'm starving."

We helped ourselves to chicken casserole, salad, pizza, and lots of other goodies. In the corner of the room was a smaller table that held a large chocolate sheet cake decorated with white frosting and pink bows. Written across it were pink letters that spelled CONGRATULATIONS.

After lunch, Mrs. Baker asked for everyone to sit on one of the chairs in the living room to watch my mom open her gifts.

Mom sat down next to a huge stack of presents.

She motioned to me and said, "Shelly, will you hand the gifts over?"

"Sure!"

After each gift I heard, "There's a lot more available for babies now than there used to be," or "Isn't that cute?" or "What will they think of next?"

Mrs. Baker, who was sitting next to Mom, wrote the name of the gift on the back of each card.

As this was all going on, there were plenty of questions for Mom. Wherever we go, people always asked the same things:

"What's the baby's name?"

"Have you seen a picture of her yet?"

"Where in China is the orphanage?"

"How will you know where to go when you get there?"

And the answers always were the same:

"We haven't named the baby yet."

"We receive her photo when the referral arrives."

"We won't know where the orphanage is until we get the referral."

"We'll be traveling with a group of people who will also be adopting a child. There will be guides meeting us at the airport to take us around."

Looking at the stack of gifts, I whispered to Stephanie, "This baby is going to have loads of clothes, toys and stuffed animals. I won't need to share any of my things with her."

"Yeah, maybe she'll share her stuff with you!"

When the party was over, Dad and Uncle Charlie arrived to carry everything back to the house. As some of the neighbors were leaving, Mom said, "Thank you so much. I live in such a great neighborhood."

Grandma, Aunt Carol, and Stephanie came back to the house with us. Grandma decided to reopen all the gifts in order to show them off to Dad, Grandpa, and Uncle Charlie.

It's funny watching Grandma. For the past two months, she's picked up this or that for the baby.

"It's on sale so I couldn't pass it up," was what she announced every time she arrived with a large shopping bag. Not only did she bring something over for the baby, she usually had a gift for me, too. This baby thing has turned out to be a pretty good deal!

Chapter Eight
A Decision Is Made

I was in the garage shoveling out the winter slush. It was a job I hated, but still had to do. I heard the mailman's car stop at our mailbox. I ran out and he handed me a letter. I looked at the envelope and saw it was from the adoption agency.

I ran into the house as fast as I could and gave the mail to Mom saying, "It's arrived!"

"Well, let's open it and see what it's about." Mom read it from top to bottom without saying a word.

"So what does it say?" I asked.

"The Chinese authorities received all of our papers. We have another seven or eight months to wait for the referral."

"Seven or eight months? That's so long." I protested.

Dad came into the room to see what all the excitement was about, and Mom handed the letter over to him.

"Dad," I asked, "what do you think we should name

the baby?"

"Hmm, that's a good question. "Do you have any suggestions?"

"I think the name should have something to do with China, don't you?"

Mom picked up the letter, reread it, and then filed it in her folder. "Maybe we can go to the library this afternoon and see if there's a book on Chinese names and their meanings."

"Can we?"

"We're not doing anything today. Let's do it!"

"You two can. I'm staying home to watch the game on TV."

After lunch we drove to the library to do just that. The librarian pointed out a book that showed common names from different countries, and we found the section on China. As I strummed through the pages, one name stood out.

"What about Ju? The name means Chrysanthemum. Here it says girls in China are often named after flowers."

"That's a possibility," Mom answered. "I like this one—Bao. It means precious treasure. She'll be a treasure."

"Naah, she won't like it when she gets older," I said as I wrinkled my nose.

We continued to search the book. I pointed to another name. "What about Chenguang? It means morning light."

"Uh huh, but maybe we should find one that's easier to say since she'll be living over here. What about Ting?"

"Ting? What does that mean?" I asked.

"Moon."

"Moon? Don't think so."

We spent over an hour trying to come up with the right name. We found Ai (loving), Buju (semi-precious stone), and Ruolan (orchid).

Nothing clicked. Either I liked it and Mom didn't, or she liked it and I didn't. The one thing we did agree on is choosing a name wasn't going to be as easy as we first thought. We wanted the name to be a part of her heritage, but easy to say.

Coming into the house, we found Dad still watching basketball on TV. He looked up from the game and asked, "So do we have a name?"

"We saw many names but nothing jumped out at us," Mom said as she hung her coat in the closet, and flopped into the overstuffed chair next to the TV.

"Interesting. Well, I have an idea," Dad said puffing out his chest.

"What is it?" I asked half heartedly. I wasn't expecting too much here.

"I think we should name her Mei. It sounds like May which is easy to say and remember, and it means plum blossom."

Mom and I looked at each other.

"I think I like it," I said to Mom.

"Mei? Plum blossom? You know, Shelly, you did say girls are often named after flowers. Plum blossoms are beautiful—certainly a sign of new life. How did you come up with that, Steve?"

"It just popped into my head. Actually, Mei's a common name in China."

"Shelly," Mom called out, "I just thought of something. Plums are purple and we decorated her room purple!"

"You're right," I said as I kicked my shoes off. "That's a sign!"

"What do you think?" Mom asked Dad.

"I think that's what we should call her," Dad said.

"Mei has my vote, too," agreed Mom. "So Mei it is."

"Dad, I can't believe we spent all afternoon at the

library researching names only to decide on nothing. Then we get home and you come up with a name—just like that," I said as I snapped my finger and thumb together.

After deciding Mei would be the baby's name, I called Amy to see what she thought. I told her about everything that happened, and how it was my father who came up with a name we all liked.

"That is so funny," she laughed.

I hung up the phone and thought, "My little sister will be called Mei. I like the way that sounds."

Chapter Nine
A Sleepover

It's always fun leaving school and going to a friend's house for a sleepover. Instead of getting off the bus at my house, I stayed on until Amy's stop.

"Mom, we're here!" Amy called out as we walked through the front door.

"My mom has Fridays off from work," Amy explained as we made our way to the kitchen. Mrs. Klein was a pharmacist at the neighborhood drug store. Whenever my mom and I went in there, we saw her behind the counter wearing her long white coat as she filled prescriptions. Today she was in the kitchen wearing a green apron making spaghetti sauce.

"Hi, girls! Shelly, I'm glad you're able to spend the night. Your mom dropped off your sleeping bag and clothes this afternoon."

"Thanks for inviting me, Mrs. Klein."

"We're going up to my room, Mom. Call us when

dinner's ready."

"We'll be eating earlier today because we're going to the skating rink. Do you like to ice skate, Shelly?"

"I love it," I called over my shoulder as I followed Amy up to her room.

At the skating rink Amy's dad warned us, "Now girls, I've only ice skated once before in my life. This isn't something I feel comfortable doing."

Amy and I looked at each other and giggled.

"Does this mean you're going to be laughing at me?"

"I'll help you, Daddy," Gracie said.

Amy and I slipped on our skates and immediately raced around the rink to the music that played from the loud speakers. As we completed our third trip around, I spotted Amy's dad attempting to stand up on his skates. One arm waved frantically in the air while the other held onto the railing.

"Amy, look at your dad. You can tell he's new at this." I tried very hard to keep from laughing. "Gracie is also having a bit of trouble," I said as I noticed her clinging onto Mrs. Klein's hand.

"My dad won't be any help. He has all he can do to stay standing himself."

We waved at them as we flew past.

"How do you girls do that?" Mr. Klein yelled and then fell onto the ice.

"Amy, don't you just love skating? Won't it be fun to come by ourselves when we're older, and meet up with friends from school?"

"Yeah, without parents," Amy said as she watched her father painfully raise himself from the ice only to fall again.

After two hours of skating, we returned to Amy's house. I overheard her dad tell Mrs. Klein he's never doing that again—something about nearly breaking his neck.

We changed into our pajamas, grabbed a bowl of popcorn and a glass of soda, and settled in to watch a TV special on pandas.

"Pandas! I love pandas. They're my favorite animal," Gracie yelled as she jumped onto the couch and spilled some of the popcorn.

."Gracie, go to bed."

"Not now, Amy. I'll go after this show."

"Mommmm, tell Gracie to leave!"

"I just want to watch this show, Mom," pleaded Gracie.

"Girls, stop fighting," warned Mrs. Klein. "Gracie, go to bed after the show is over."

Gracie looked over at us with this "I won" look on her face. Amy snarled.

On TV a reporter and zookeeper were standing outside a habitat that was made just for the panda bears.

The reporter asked, "I understand these bears arrived over here from China in December 2000."

"Yes," said the zookeeper, "they're a gift to the United States but only for ten years. Then they must be sent back."

"They're so cute," Gracie yelled.

"Shhh—I want to hear this," warned Amy.

Gracie threw a pillow at her sister and complained, "How come you can talk?"

Amy ignored her as she continued to watch TV. I certainly hope my new sister and I will get along better than Gracie and Amy.

The zookeeper continued to explain how these were the second pair of bears given to the zoo. Back in the 1970's, Ling-Ling and Hsing-Hsing were the first, but they have since died. "The pandas you see here are Mei Xiang and Tian Tian. They were born in 1998 and 1997. Mei Xiang's name means 'beautiful fragrance' while Tian Tian's name means 'more and more'."

"Amy, look at the cub," I said as he lumbered into view. "He's adorable."

The zookeeper went on to tell us about the cub. "This is Mei Xiang's and Tian Tian's cub who was born in 2005. We had a contest to name him, and the name Tai Shan won. It means 'Peaceful Mountain'."

"I want a panda!" Gracie yelled.

"Shhh," Amy warned. Turning her attention away from her sister, Amy looked over at me and asked, "Will you see any pandas while you're in China?"

"Maybe, even though we'll be busy with the adoption thing, my dad said we should be there long enough to see some of the sights."

"Lucky you," said Amy. "Someday I wanna go to China."

"Me, too," copied Gracie.

"Not with me," Amy shot back as she turned the TV off. "Show's over. Go to bed."

"Alright—you're always so mean when you have someone here."

"I don't bother you when your friends are over."

Gracie picked up her pillow and trudged out of the room. Part of me felt sorry for her.

With the lights off, we settled into the warmth of our sleeping bags. The house was quiet. The tick tock of the antique clock in the hallway could be heard all through the house. I started thinking about Mei. What's she doing? Is she even born yet? If she is, how old is she? What are her days like? Has she ever been sick? Does she feel alone? Is she afraid? I'm hoping she's not. I secretly whispered to her, "Hold on, Mei. We're coming for you. Just hold on."

Chapter Ten
Meeting Other Families

After my parents picked me up from Amy's, we drove to Mr. and Mrs. Presley's house. The Presleys adopted a baby from China two years ago, and they were having a get together with other families who adopted. Mom told me they meet at each other's homes every other month.

"Not only do the parents share information, but the kids get to know and play with other kids who were adopted from China."

"Why do they do that?" I asked.

"It's all part of their agreement with the Chinese government. You know, to keep alive Chinese traditions. This way the children will know about the country they came from."

"Oh, so why are we going? We don't have the baby yet."

"The Presleys heard we're in the process so they invited

us to join their group," Dad explained as our car stopped at the red light.

"She thought it would help if we met other people who've adopted," Mom added.

"I wish I didn't have to go. This is going to be so boring. Why couldn't I just stay at Amy's while you guys go?"

"No, Shelly. This is a family activity and all three of us are doing this together," Dad said as he turned the car onto the highway.

When we arrived, we found three other families sitting in the family room talking—the Hoffmans, the Boyds, and the Averys. They seemed excited to meet us and asked lots of questions.

"Have you seen a picture of the baby yet?" Mrs. Presley asked. Mrs. Presley was a tall, thin lady with brown curly hair. She seemed to be always smiling and cracking jokes.

"No, but we received word our papers reached China," Mom answered. "Now we're waiting for the referral to come through."

"That part took forever," Mrs. Presley said as she patted her little girl on the head. "This is Emily. She's three. We plan on starting the process again to receive another child from China so she'll have a sister."

"That's wonderful," said Mrs. Hoffman. The Hoffmans have two children from China. One is a four year old girl named Kay, and the other is a two year old boy named Thomas.

"It's not easy adopting a boy from China because of that 'one child law'," Mr. Hoffman told us. "But Thomas had many health problems so the government agreed to let him leave the country."

The Hoffmans were friendly but quiet people. Mrs. Hoffman, much shorter than Mrs. Presley, wore her hair twisted in a braid. I found myself fascinated by it and wished I knew her better so I could ask her how she did that. Mr. Hoffman wore glasses and had the beginnings of a beard. I wasn't quite sure if that's how he wanted to look or if he just didn't have time to shave today.

"In the 18 months we've had Thomas, he's had several operations to correct his cleft palate," said Mrs. Hoffman.

"What's a cleft palate?" I asked.

"That's when the roof of your mouth doesn't develop. Instead it's open which makes it hard to speak and eat," explained Mrs. Hoffman.

"Really? That sounds gross."

"Shelly?" Mom warned as she gave me the evil eye. You know, all moms can give those really good.

I started thinking how Thomas was lucky to be adopted by the Hoffmans. I felt bad for the kids who never received any help.

The Boyds and the Averys had other kids besides their adopted children. The Boyds had a daughter, Chelsea, who was my age and a son, Jon, who was twelve. Their four year old daughter, Kim, came over from China when she was ten months old.

At first I felt out of place amongst all these new people. Meeting Natalie Avery changed all that. Natalie's friendly personality melted away any anxiety I might have had. Like me, she was ten and in fifth grade. She had a long, blonde pony tail that stuck out from under a baseball cap. I felt a little shy because she and Chelsea knew each other so well.

But after Natalie invited me to join them in the board game they were playing, our conversation became easier. I felt I had more in common with Natalie since we were both the only child in the family when our parents decided to adopt.

She warned me, "When the baby first arrives, it can be a little weird. Everyone wants to see her."

"How old is your sister?"

"Lin's four. She was about 15 months when she came to live with us."

"Were you happy about it?" I asked Natalie.

"I was, but she had all these problems with walking."

"What kind of problems?" I asked as I moved my place marker around the board.

"She just wouldn't do it. We tried to help her, but she cried and raised her arms to be carried."

"Why wasn't she walking?" Chelsea asked.

"We discovered the orphanage kept her in a crib much of the day so she never tried to walk. Another problem was she couldn't understand English and we couldn't speak Chinese."

"Wow!" I said. "Now she walks and talks like the other kids."

"Yeah, some orphanages are better than others. I hope your new sister doesn't have any problems getting used to you."

"I hope not either. Maybe it won't be as hard because she'll be younger," I answered as I took my turn shaking the dice.

I saw Lin and Kim chasing each other in a circle made by going from the kitchen to the dining room to the living room and back to the kitchen again. They were having fun. Their screams could be heard echoing throughout the house until Mrs. Avery came in and put a stop to their chasing game.

After lunch, it was time for the cultural lesson the host family puts together.

Mrs. Presley announced, "Okay everyone. We're going to try a little calligraphy."

"That sounds like fun," I whispered to my mom.

"See, I told you this would be good."

We all left what we were doing and went downstairs into the basement. It was finished off with paneling, had some furniture, and a soft, blue rug in one part of the room. In the other part of the cellar there were three tables set up with several folding chairs. Mrs. Presley placed drawing paper, brushes, and black ink on the longer table.

Mr. Presley held up one of the samples and said, "In the past, Chinese children learned this style of writing using brushes and ink, but now they use pens and pencils like us. Here you see how one is done."

I picked up a sample and looked at the graceful lines that flowed across the page. Mrs. Presley told us each group of brush strokes represented either an idea or a thing.

"Sometimes calligraphy is used to explain a painting with black Chinese characters written right across the picture," Mrs. Presley explained.

We sat down with a brush and some paper. The younger kids stood and watched as we copied the samples Mrs. Presley had there for us. The time went by very quickly. Just as I started to get the hang of it, we had to leave.

"Can we get supplies at the craft shop and do this at home?" I asked my mom.

"Sounds like a plan," promised Mom.

Gathering by the door, Mrs. Boyd announced, "It's our turn to have the next get together which should be in June. Would it be okay with all of you if we met on the second Saturday in July instead?"

"Sounds good," Mr. Presley said. Jeff Presley was very tall and didn't talk as much as Mrs. Presley. When he was having a conversation, it always seemed to be about golf. Which course he played on and what his handicap was. My dad doesn't golf, but he seemed interested in what Mr. Presley had to say. Mr. Presley even offered to take Dad out on the course.

"June is such a busy month," continued Mrs. Boyd, "with baseball and all the activities at the end of the school year."

The Boyds were very involved in activities. Everyone in the family did many things. Later, I heard my mom mention to my dad, "I don't know how David and Sandy keep everything straight. It sounds like someone needs to be somewhere all the time."

"So, Bob and Patty, is July okay with you for our next get together?" Mrs. Boyd asked the Averys.

"That's fine with us, Sandy," Mrs. Avery said.

Mrs. Boyd added, "We're planning a Chinese dinner. When the day gets closer, I'll give each of you a call. You can let me know the dish you are bringing and from which region it originated."

"Kathy, Steve, and Shelly, we hope you join our group," said Mrs. Presley.

"We'd love to," my mom said. "Today was such fun. Thanks for including us."

Everyone waved goodbye as we pulled away in our car.

"You know, that's something all countries understand," I said to my parents.

"What's that?" Dad asked.

"Someone waving goodbye."

Chapter Eleven
The Dragon Boat Festival

What's special about May 1st? It's the spring weather. Amy and I always enjoy the day we take our bikes out of winter storage and ride them around the block. Grownups say the year goes by fast, but for us kids, it doesn't.

After months of cold weather, we look forward to these spring days. At school we stare at the clock waiting for recess. On the playground, groups of kids play ball, swing, or chase each other. Nobody likes to hear the sound of the whistle calling everyone back into the building.

Today was no different. We returned to our room energized and ready to read the new book Mrs. Standish had placed on our desks.

"Class, this book is about spring rituals different countries have. Today we will find out about a few of them."

Jeff, a la medieval boy, read how the first of May was

always celebrated with children hanging a small bouquet of flowers on someone's doorknob.

"Mrs. Standish, I remember weaving a basket and making tissue flowers in first grade. I put the basket on my doorknob at home, rang the bell, and hid behind a bush. When my mom answered the door, I jumped out and surprised her."

"That's exactly how it works, Shelly," said Mrs. Standish.

Everyone who was in Mrs. Adam's first grade room had similar stories to tell.

Sarah read the section telling about the celebration of spring in Europe. One custom had to do with the Maypole.

"Christina, did you have a Maypole where you lived?" asked Mrs. Standish. Christina moved here from a small town outside of Munich, Germany last year.

"Ja, we had a Maypole near this uh little park by my house. In May, streamers were attached to the top of the pole. People held onto these streamers and danced around the pole. In Germany we celebrated the day with music and food."

In China, we learned about the Dragon Boat Festival that took place on the fifth day of the fifth month of the Chinese calendar. An actual dragon boat race marked this spring celebration. Just like in Europe, eating used up much of the day as people enjoyed rice dumplings wrapped in lotus leaves.

Mark, the smartest kid in the class, raised his hand and asked, "What's the story behind the festival?"

"Well, how about reading the next paragraph for that answer, Mark?" suggested Mrs. Standish.

Mark read, "It all had to do with a man named Qu Yuan. He loved his country and became upset when the enemy took over. So Qu Yuan killed himself by jumping into the Li River. During the festival, the dragon boat race and the noise of the drums scare away the fish. The rice dumplings are thrown in the water to feed the fish so they won't bother Qu Yuan's body."

"That's nasty," yelled out Jeff.

"It's all part of their culture," explained Mrs. Standish. "The same is true with dragons. Did you know there are four very important animals that are important in Chinese legends? Besides the dragon, there's the phoenix, the turtle, and the unicorn."

"What's a phoenix?" asked Amy.

"You don't know what a phoenix is?" laughed Mark.

"Mark, let's not be rude to Amy. Instead of making fun, why don't you explain what it is."

"Sorry, Amy. It's a legendary bird. When it comes to the end of its life, it will burn itself to death. Then the phoenix will rise from its ashes as a young bird." Mark raised his arms over his head to make it appear as though he would grab something.

"Thank you, Mark," Mrs. Standish interrupted. "Actually, these four creatures helped P'an Ku make the universe. Now let's continue with the story. Jason, how about reading the next paragraph."

Having the reputation of being the class daydreamer, Jason didn't disappoint us as he sat up straight trying to find his place in the book. I had a hunch Mrs. Standish purposely called on him to pull him back to Earth. Erin saw him struggling and quietly pointed to the paragraph on the page.

Jason gave a smile of gratitude and read, "P'an Ku, the first man according to Chinese legend, supposedly came from an egg. Inside this egg could be found everything needed to make the world. P'an Ku had two horns, two tusks, and a hairy body."

"That's awesome," blurted out Jeffrey.

"But it gets better," said Mrs. Standish. "Shelly, finish it up."

"Okay," I said as I cleared my throat. "P'an Ku grew ten feet each day. As he grew he separated the earth and the sky within the egg. He also separated the many opposites of the universe such as wet and dry, hot and cold, male and female, Yin and Yang. Inside the egg he made the first humans. It took 18,000 years, but finally the egg hatched and P'an Ku died from all his hard work."

"What happened next?" Danny wanted to know.

"After he died," Mrs. Standish said, "his skin became the soil, his hair became the trees, his bones turned into mountains, his sweat turned into rain, and his blood became the sea. The sun and moon came from both his eyes. His voice became the thunder and his breath became the wind."

"Awesome," Jason yelled out again. "Did that really happen?"

Mrs. Standish smiled and said, "It's all part of Chinese mythology. Long ago, people didn't have scientific knowledge to explain things they didn't understand. So they used these characters in mythical stories to explain what they couldn't."

"The Greeks and Romans have myths, too." added Sarah.

"Yes, Sarah, and more people know about Roman and Greek Mythology than Chinese."

"They had great imaginations," I added.

"You're right, Shelly, they did. Now let's check out your imagination." Mrs. Standish walked over to the back of the room. "Here we have a variety of craft materials you can use for your next activity."

Mrs. Standish pointed a table piled high with assorted construction paper, crayons, glue, tissue paper, and other art supplies.

"There are three different projects to choose from—a Maypole diorama, a basket of May flowers, or a dragon boat. Have some fun with it!"

"No problem deciding this one," I said to Amy. "I'm making the boat." And for a brief moment, I could feel the magic of the dragon.

Chapter Twelve
Spring Fever

Spring continued to make its appearance at its usual slow pace. Daylight stayed a little longer, and the honking sounds of the geese no longer could be heard as they journeyed northward. I enjoyed this time of year. I loved not wearing a closet full of clothes every time I went outside. Trees blossomed and baby leaves covered up the once bare branches. The earth stretched and yawned in April, but it woke up in May.

On mornings like this, I found it hard going to school and returning home only to have homework assignments to do. How I wanted to be free from it all! As I sat at my desk in my bedroom, I gazed out the window wishing I could be somewhere else. Mom told me I had a bad case of spring fever.

I heard the doorbell and welcomed the interruption. I looked downstairs and saw Mrs. Presley holding a large book under her arm. She told Mom it was a Lifebook. My curiosity got the best of me, so I went downstairs to say hello.

Mrs. Presley motioned to me and said, "Shelly, you're just in time to see Emily's Lifebook."

"What's that?" I asked.

"Sometimes families who adopt a child put one of these together while they're waiting for further news of the baby. I brought it over to show your mom. Come look and see!"

We sat down on the couch and Mrs. Presley slowly opened the book. On the first couple of pages, she grouped pictures of their house and family members.

The next section had information on Emily's adoption. There were the letters the Presleys received from the adoption agency, including Emily's referral picture. Mrs. Presley proudly pointed to the certificate that proved Emily's American citizenship.

"This is a copy. The real one is in a safety deposit box at the bank." Mrs. Presley turned to the next page. "This shows our family getting ready for Emily's arrival—photos of a baby shower, a list of the gifts she received, and Emily's room before and after it was decorated."

"Cool," I said as I looked at everything.

On the next three pages, I spotted a copy of their air itinerary, plane ticket stubs, and pictures of the hotels they stayed in while in China. She saved everything.

"Where in China were you?" asked Mom.

"Oh, those photos are of us in Beijing."

"Beijing? Where's that?" I asked.

"It's a large city in China where many of the adopting families fly into," Mrs. Presley explained.

"Hey, I saw this on a large poster in the school library. What is it?" I asked.

"That's the Great Wall of China," Mrs. Presley told me.

Mom said, "Susan, I heard the Wall's so big the

astronauts can see it from space."

"Yeah, most people who travel to China want to see the Great Wall," said Mrs. Presley.

"Will we see it when we're there?" I asked Mom.

"I hope so. You can't go to China and not visit the Great Wall!"

"Look at all the people in the streets."

"Yeah, that shows how crowded China is," Mom said. "Check out all the cars and bikes."

"Shelly," Mrs. Presley said, "you should try to find out as much as you can about China before you go. Then when you get there, it'll be more interesting to you."

"Actually everyone in my class has to do a research project and then give an oral report. I'm doing mine on China."

"When's that due?" asked Mom.

"In a couple of weeks—it's going to be a large part of our Language Arts grade."

"Have you started working on it?" Mom asked.

"Not yet, soon. Do we have a Lifebook for Mei?"

"No, but we need to put something together before she arrives. We'll be busy once she gets here."

I turned the page of Emily's Lifebook and saw a letter that was written by one of the nurses at the orphanage. She described Emily as a very sweet baby. The letter explained only a little about how she got to the orphanage. It mentioned her family was poor and they weren't able to take care of her.

I saw maps and brochures of the places where the Presleys went while they waited to get the okay to return to the United States with the baby.

"Susan, is that Chinese money?" Mom asked Mrs. Presley.

"Yeah, it's called renminbi—written as RMB. It stands

for the 'people's currency.' Just like our currency is the dollar; the Chinese have the yuan. Here's a jiao and these are fens."

"This is confusing," I groaned.

Mrs. Presley said, "You know how we have ten dimes and they make a dollar? Well, in China, ten jiao make one yuan and ten fens make one jiao."

"Oh, so if the yuan was like our dollar, would the jiao be like our dime and the fen be like our penny?"

Mrs. Presley shook her head. "That's a good way to compare it, but their values are not the same."

I was not completely sure what she meant by that until my mom explained we wouldn't be able to buy the same amount with a yuan as we could with a dollar.

"Actually, Shelly, one yuan is only worth about 13 cents. So you would need about eight yuans to purchase what one dollar could buy."

"And that amount is always changing because the world's currencies are always changing," said Mrs. Presley.

"Just like the price of gas," said Mom.

I stared at the money in the Lifebook. I noticed the Great Wall of China on one side of the juan, and a picture of a man and woman on the other side. Plus there were all these Chinese letters written on it.

"It looks like play money, but probably our dollar looks like play money to them."

Mom asked, "Was it hard using this currency when you bought something?"

"Well, let's say I felt like I was a six year old closely looking at each bill while trying to figure out what I had to give the clerk. But after a few days, I got the hang of it."

"Maybe we should get some Chinese money and practice before going over there," Mom suggested as she examined the money.

"That certainly would help," agreed Mrs. Presley. "When we first got to Beijing, Jeff and I went into a small shop to buy some post cards. I could sense the clerk's amusement over our clumsiness as we handed over our money to pay for the cards."

I turned the page of the Lifebook and saw some photos of their plane ride home, and everyone waiting at the airport for Emily's arrival. One photo showed Emily's Uncle Rob with a huge sign that said, WELCOME TO THE FAMILY, EMILY.

"We had a big party two weeks after we returned from China," Mrs. Presley explained. "Everyone wanted to see the new baby."

"Is this the party?" I asked pointing to several pictures showing different people holding Emily.

"Yeah, it was a huge celebration."

Adoption announcements followed and a snippet of Emily's hair was placed in a small envelope and attached to one of the later pages. At the back of the book Mrs. Presley included some newspaper articles she found on China right around the time of Emily's arrival.

Mom laid the book on the table and invited Mrs. Presley into the kitchen for a cup of coffee. I stayed in the living room to look through the Lifebook another time. I saw this picture of Emily getting her shots right after she arrived in the United States. She didn't look too happy there.

Mom and Mrs. Presley returned to the living room with their coffee and saw me still looking at the book.

"Shelly," Mom asked, "what do you think? Are you interested in putting together a Lifebook for Mei?"

"Sure, it'll be fun. There's so much we can put in it already—pictures of her room, the baby shower, and our neighborhood."

"Don't forget the pictures we took of our support family gatherings," Mom added.

After Mrs. Presley left, we decided to go to the library over the weekend and check out books on China.

"I need to find information for both Mei's Lifebook, and my research project," I said.

"There's an old Chinese saying for that—kill two birds with one stone," Mom teased as she left the room.

What happened next was amazing. A whole new energy entered my body and cured me of my spring fever!

Chapter Thirteen
A Fascinating Country

I spent the whole weekend writing my report on China. I used library books and the internet for my research. I never knew much about that country. I knew it was far away, the people used chopsticks, and they ate a lot of rice and dumplings. But after researching for this report, I felt like an expert.

"Shelly, you have a phone call. It's Amy," Mom yelled up to me.

I picked up the phone. "Hello?"

"Hi, Shelly. Want to go to a movie this afternoon?"

"I can't. I'm still working on my report."

"Oh, how's it coming?"

"Much better now that I'm into it. Hey, did you know China is the third largest country in the world?"

"No, who are numbers one and two?"

"Canada and Russia—China also has the largest population," I added.

"Yeah, that's why they have that one child law you were telling me about, right?"

"Right."

"How come so much is known about China?" Amy asked.

"It has the longest recorded history," I explained.

"Even before the days of CNN?" joked Amy.

"Yeah, now everybody knows about everything. No secrets today!" We both laughed at that one.

Did China ever have a king?" Amy asked.

"No, an emperor. He was kinda like a king because when he died, his oldest son took his place. These families of rulers were called dynasties."

"Sweet," said Amy.

"Wish I could go to the movies. What are ya gonna see?"

"The Explosion of Spiders—it just came out. Maybe I'll call Erin and see if she wants to go."

"Okay, next time. I really have to get this thing done."

I hung up the phone and went downstairs to get a snack. All that researching makes a person hungry.

"What did Amy want, Shelly?" asked Mom.

"She wanted to know if I could go to the movies, but I told her I had to finish my report."

"That's right, your report. Shelly, have you read anything about the Silk Road?" my mom asked.

I poured a glass of juice and helped myself to a bowl of chips.

"It was mentioned in one of my books, but I didn't get why they called it the Silk Road."

"Oh, well...it seems the city of Xi'an connected central Asia with many parts of Europe. Caravans of people would pass by as they brought horses and gold with them to exchange for silk. So from that it became known as the

Silk Road."

My dad listened as Mom explained all this to me.

"I think Xi'an is an industrial city now," he added. They make mostly textile cloths."

"Dad, have you ever heard of the Terracotta Warriors? They're in that Xi'an place."

"I have. That's probably one of the most visited sites in China after the Great Wall, and it's only been since the mid 1970's that we knew about them."

"Really? Who found them?" Mom asked.

"From what I can remember, there was a farmer digging a well when he uncovered broken pieces of pottery. He told some government officials about this and archeologists were sent out to see if there was anything else buried on the site."

"Is that when they found them?" I asked.

"Yeah, they were surprised to uncover not only the warriors, but also clay horses, and chariots."

"Other things have been uncovered before. Why was this such a big deal?" I asked.

Dad walked over to the book shelf and pulled out a travel guide to China. He opened it to the section on Xi'an and showed me a picture. "Look here. These figures aren't small. They're life-sized. Plus, look how many! There's about 7000 officers and soldiers altogether."

"Seven thousand? Life-sized?" I couldn't believe it.

"Yeah, they're holding swords and spears," Dad continued. "Some of them are driving horses attached to life-sized chariots."

"That's huge! Who made all that?" I asked.

"The emperor, Qin Shi Huangdi, had them built to impersonate his imperial guard. The warriors even had their own facial expressions," Dad explained.

"Why?"

"Qin wanted to be protected from his enemies even after his death. It was all to be part of his tomb. That's why it was buried."

"Can we see this?"

"I hope so, but no promises," warned Dad.

"We'll have to see what our travel itinerary looks like," Mom reminded me.

"One thing I'm certain about is the more I find out about China, the more excited I am about going," I announced as I turned to another page.

"It seems like an amazing place," Mom said as she looked over my shoulder at the pictures. "Sounds like you're doing a great job on your report. You'll have to write everything up in a story and we'll put it in Mei's Lifebook."

"Look! Here's something about the Great Wall," I said as I pointed to another picture. "We saw that in Emily's Lifebook."

"That's probably one of the most recognizable sights in the world," said Mom. "The book says the wall is about 4000 miles long."

"And to give you an idea why that's such a big deal, the distance between New York and California is around 3000 miles," Dad pointed out.

"Really? Did the Chinese people make it?"

"Yeah, the Wall was made by millions of Chinese. Probably most of them were slaves. It took several centuries to get it done."

"Was it built to protect the country?" I asked.

"Ah uh, the Emperor wanted to protect his empire from enemies who tried to invade," Dad told me. "The Wall was also used as an elevated highway."

I looked at the book to read what it said about the Wall. "Dad, did you know the Emperor wanted the wall to be six horses wide at the top and eight horses wide at the bottom? That's big."

"Really?" Mom asked.

I went on, "Ah huh, he also wanted it to be five men high. Whoa! That's tall. It's strange how they measured things by horses and men instead of feet and yards."

Mom opened the window to let the warm breeze into the room. "They used what everyone was familiar with, Shelly. There was no standard measurement back then."

"The Boyds saw the Wall on their trip over there," Dad said. They told me it was made of bricks, mud, and stone, and purposely made to wind along the countryside like a dragon."

"Dragons again. Why were they so important? They aren't even real animals. Just pretend, like unicorns."

Dad explained, "It's because dragons were thought to be sacred. They look mean, but the people thought they brought good luck, strength, and wisdom."

Mom added, "At first dragons were allowed to be shown only on the clothing of emperors. Later they appeared on dishes and were used as decorations."

"And can be seen as a wall winding its way across China," I laughed.

Chapter Fourteen
Morning Jitters

I woke up this morning before the alarm went off. I do that whenever I'm worried about something. Today's the day of my oral report. I wouldn't be nervous if I could read it, but Mrs. Standish does not want us to do it that way. Instead, she showed us how to list key words on an index card and to use those words as a reminder of what we want to say. So if we are stuck, we look for the key word on the card.

I walked into the kitchen and saw my dad as he was about to rush out the door for work.

"Hey, good luck on that report, Shelly."

"Thanks."

"What's the matter?" Dad asked as he was taking one last swallow of his coffee.

"Oh, nothing."

"Nothing? Looks like something's on your mind."

"It's just...I don't know...my report. I hope I remember

what I'm supposed to say."

"You'll do okay. You practiced it enough. That's half the battle. If you're prepared, everything will fall into place when you start talking."

"What if it doesn't?" I asked.

My mom walked in and caught the drift of our conversation. "Look, Shelly," she said. "Dad's right. Only the kids who spent little time on their project should worry. You're prepared; so have fun talking about China."

With their reassurance, I reluctantly got on the bus and waited for Amy's stop. At least she'll understand how I feel. She gave her report on Friday.

"So are you ready for today?" Amy asked as soon as she sat down next to me.

"I guess. At least my parents think I am. I hope I don't get so nervous I puke."

Amy laughed. "You won't puke. It's scary just before your turn. You get all these butterflies in your stomach and your mouth dries up. But as soon as you start talking, things get better."

Amy searched through her backpack and pulled out what appeared to be a piece of candy covered in gold foil. "Here's a mint. Pop one of these a few minutes before your turn. It takes the dryness out of your mouth. That's what my mom told me to do and it worked."

"Thanks," I said as I stuck it in my pocket. By the way, you did a great job on your report. I'll bet you'll get an A on it."

"Really?"

"Yeah, you didn't even look nervous."

"You're kidding. I was petrified. It's very scary to stand up and talk in front of the class. Why do teachers torture us and make us do stuff like that?"

"My parents told me it's normal to be afraid whenever I

try something new. But the more I do it, the easier it becomes," I explained.

"Really?"

"That's what they say, and I think they might be right. Remember that high dive at Morningside Heights Pool? Last summer I climbed to the top and stood there for the longest time because I was too afraid to jump."

"Yeah, I remember. The line behind you got sooo long."

"I know. It was embarrassing when I saw all those kids behind me, but I was frozen to the board."

"And you couldn't change your mind and turn back because of that line," Amy added.

"I was so scared. Finally, I took a deep breath and jumped off. Before I knew it, I was in the water swimming to the side of the pool."

"And then you did it again."

"I did. And again, and again, and again. After awhile, it wasn't scary at all. It became fun."

"I see what you're getting at," Amy said. "If we give enough reports, we won't be afraid when we talk in front of people."

"I think so. Anyhow, that's what happened to me jumping off the high dive."

"For me, it was riding the roller coaster!" Amy said as she got up from the seat to get off the bus. "Come on, we're here."

I looked out the window and saw kids leaving their buses and slowly filing into school.

"We're here?" I groaned. "How I wish I didn't have to do this!"

Amy put her hand on my shoulder and said, "Keep repeating these words—the high dive, the high dive."

I walked into the classroom and noticed Mrs. Moreno,

the substitute teacher. She subbed for Mrs. Standish before, but today was different. I give my report today. What do I do now? Should I tell Mrs. Moreno I'm supposed to give a report?

"Mrs. Standish's son is sick and she has to take him to the doctor's," Mrs. Moreno told us. "She'll be in school tomorrow. According to the note she left me, two of you are scheduled to give an oral report today. Who are you?"

Both Erin and I raised our hands.

"Mrs. Standish wants to hear them. She asked me to tell you she's sorry about this, but to be prepared to give the report tomorrow."

I felt the butterflies immediately disappear—like magic. My hands stopped shaking, and my head became clearer. A sudden peacefulness came over me as I settled into the morning's first assignment. I've been spared. All was right with the world again until something occurred to me.

"Great," I whispered to Amy. "I get to do this morning all over again tomorrow."

"Lucky you," Amy said as she tilted her head to the side and gave a silly smile.

"Not funny!" I turned around and looked at Erin. She raised her eyebrows and scrunched up her nose. Her thoughts were the same as mine. Our sentencing had only been postponed.

Chapter Fifteen
The Day of Terror

I stumbled off the bus with those butterflies back in tow, and walked to my classroom not knowing if I wanted to see the substitute teacher again. There was no getting out of this. I needed to be done with this report.

As soon as I walked in, I spotted Mrs. Standish in the back of the room watering the plants that sat wilting on the windowsill. The day of terror arrived.

Language Arts wasn't until 10:15 so I wrestled those butterflies all through Math and Reading. After a quick snack break, I heard Mrs. Standish say, "Boys and girls, it's time to get back to your seats. Shelly will be the first one to give her report."

Amy was right. I was dry. My tongue stuck to the roof of my mouth, and I had difficulty pulling my lips apart to speak. I remembered the mint she gave me yesterday. I unwrapped it and quickly threw it into my mouth. Instantly, it helped. Thank you, Amy's mother!

I walked to the front of the room, turned to face the class, and was frozen with fear. I thought about the high dive with the long line of kids behind me. No line this time. I'm up here all alone, looking at everyone staring back at me.

I took a deep breath and said, "My research report is on China. This is a country that has more than one billion people which is about one fifth of the world's population. There's an easy way to understand that. Think about taking all the people in the world and dividing them into five equal groups. One of these groups would be just China. The rest of the world would make up the other four groups."

They listened. No one opened their desks, or doodled on their notebook, or looked out the window—they listened. Not only did they listen, they seemed interested in what I said. I started to breathe. Breathing is important when you give a report.

Before I knew it, I was done. Everyone clapped which is what we did after everyone's report.

"That was good," Amy whispered.

"You know what's crazy? I don't know what I said."

As I sat unwinding at my desk, I heard Erin's voice saying, "My report is on polar bears."

When I returned home later that afternoon, my parents asked how my report went.

"I don't know."

"You don't know?" my mom asked. "Did it go smoothly? Did you remember what to say?"

"It was so weird. Once I started talking, words flew out of my mouth. I totally lost control."

"So I take it things went well?" Dad asked.

"Mrs. Standish said I did a good job and Amy said she liked it. But...I don't remember what I said!"

"That's funny!" Mom said. "Anyway, be sure to put a

copy of the report in Mei's Lifebook. Then when she's older, you'll have to tell her how you survived your...what did you call it...your day of terror?"

"Yeah, and without remembering how I did it!" I shook my head as I walked to the refrigerator and pulled out a chocolate pudding snack. "At least it's over. Yahoo! It's over! No more jumps off the diving board!"

"No more what?" Mom asked with a confused look on her face.

"Ah nothing, inside joke."

Chapter Sixteen
Xi Shou Jian Zai Na Li?

The empty room below the church had paneled walls, cheap carpeting, and a strong smell of green pine air freshener. I attended the meeting with my parents and several other families who were adopting from China. We were there to learn some of the Chinese language.

"Having a little understanding of Chinese will be useful when we visit the country," Dad told me when we were driving to the church. "We should also have an easier time communicating with Mei if we know some words."

Mr. Chang greeted us as we sat behind the other families who arrived earlier. He was a friendly man—rather short with black glasses. Behind him stood a blackboard with a few Chinese phrases written on it. I had no idea what it all meant, but I guess that's why we're here.

Mr. Chang said, "Today we'll have the first of six lessons in Chinese. We'll start by saying a few common phrases you'll find helpful on your trip over there. Once you know them, you can practice saying them at home. For example, if you want to say 'yes' in Chinese, just say Shi. Bu shi means 'no'." A chorus of voices all went Shi and Bu shi.

Mr. Chang said, "Good Job. When you're greeting someone in the morning, you might want to say, Zao an. If it's the afternoon, say Wu an, and good night would be Wan an. So let's have everyone try that."

Once more the group could be heard saying Zao an, wan an, and wu an. Much confusion erupted as no one could remember which expression meant what.

Mr. Lewis, who was sitting in front of us, raised his hand. "Let's say I'm in the store and I want to buy something. How do I ask how much something costs?"

"Duo shao qian?"

A rumbling of voices could be heard saying, "Duo shao quan."

Mr. Chang listened to the group practice their new phrase. Then he raised his hand for everyone to be quiet.

"If you're in a restaurant (jiu lou) and you want the check, you should say, Jie zhang. That means to please bring the bill."

While I listened to the grownups practice their Chinese, I noticed a girl standing near the door. I walked over to her and said, "Hi, my name is Shelly. Is your family adopting a baby from China, too?"

"Hi, Shelly, I'm Becky. We are, but we don't know when."

"I know. We're still waiting for our referral, too."

"Will you be going over to China with your parents?" she asked.

"Yeah, they said I can go. What about you?"

"No, I have to stay with my grandmother. She's coming to our house to watch me and my brother, Sam. I kinda wish

I could go, but my mom said it would be too expensive. You're so lucky."

"Where do you go to school?" I asked.

"I'm in sixth grade at Bradley Middle School," she said. "How about you?"

"Fifth grade at Madison, but I'll be going to the middle school next fall."

"Really? Maybe I'll see you there," Becky said as she sat down in a chair.

Feeling a little relieved I might know someone there, I asked, "Do you like the middle school? I'm kinda worried about it."

"No worries. It's great! You'll have a homeroom plus a different teacher for every subject. I have Mr. Gordon for both homeroom and science. His class is lots of fun— especially the labs. We're always doing experiments and stuff."

"Experiments?" I asked. "We did this unit on water pollution. The kids in my class tested water from many different places. Then we graphed our results. It was fun!"

"Sounds like it was. I like school, but I'm excited about summer vacation," Becky said as she leaned back in her chair.

"Yeah," I agreed, "I can't wait to just hang out."

"Me, too," Becky said with a smile. "Do you have any brothers or sisters?"

"No, I'm an only child—until now. At first I wasn't happy with this adoption thing, but now I'm okay with it."

Becky offered me a little reassurance. "I like the idea of having a sister, but my brother wishes the baby was a boy. Two against one, I say!"

Right at that moment the room filled with laughter. We stopped talking as we wondered what was going on. I walked over to my mom and asked her why everyone was laughing.

"We just learned Xi shou jian zai na li."

"What does that mean?"

"It means, 'Where's the bathroom?'"

Chapter Seventeen
Summer Vacation

My alarm clock went off at seven. This is not unusual as it goes off at seven every school day. Normally I groan, stretch, pull the pillow over my head, and pretend the annoying blast of noise never happened. Today was different. I hopped out of bed and jumped into the clothes that draped over my desk chair. I was excited. Summer vacation would be starting in five hours.

I liked fifth grade and enjoyed having Mrs. Standish as my teacher. She made learning fun and the days zipped by quickly. I knew I would miss her and Madison Elementary. But those lazy, do little days of summer had too much of a lure.

Today's also the last day I'm ten. Tomorrow I'm having my birthday party with all my friends. I decided to have a summer Olympic theme with everyone arriving with their bathing suits. Yesterday Mom made up a bunch of gold medals for prizes. For lunch, Dad's making chicken kabobs on a stick. We're calling them Olympic torches! I can't wait.

Two hours later I found myself walking toward Room 233 for the last time. These halls will be missed. Madison had been the only school I've ever attended. It's so familiar. I won't know where anything is at the middle school. But neither will my friends. We'll find out together.

We cleaned out our desks and put the textbooks in piles on the large table in the back of the room. Everything else went into our backpack. The green colored pencil I was looking for a month ago was found between my math folder and my pack of tissues.

Mrs. Standish assigned us jobs. Amy and I were in charge of the library section. We cleaned up the books, taped any rips, and stacked them onto dusted shelves. Mrs. Standish wandered around the room complimenting how well we all worked together. No one fooled around. Not even Jeffrey.

"Amy, why is cleaning in school fun, while cleaning at home boring?" I asked.

"Don't know. I could never figure that out."

Just as we finished, Mrs. Standish walked over. "How are things going with the adoption, Shelly?"

"We're still waiting for the referral. We'll probably get it in the fall, and then it'll be another six weeks before we can fly to China to pick her up."

"I'll be thinking of you. What a wonderful experience it'll be not only to go to China, but to get a little sister. Your family is doing a very nice thing here."

"Thanks, Mrs. Standish."

Just as we were finishing our conversation, Mrs. Crowley, the school principal, got on the loud speaker and announced: "Buses will be called in fifteen minutes. We hope everyone has a safe and restful summer. See you in

September."

Mrs. Standish asked us to quickly get into our seats.

"Class, I want to tell you how much I enjoyed being your teacher. It's been a great year for me, and I'll miss seeing your smiling faces. I wish all of you great success in the middle school. Don't forget all of us back at Madison Elementary."

Then she slowly walked over to her desk, opened a drawer, and pulled out a stack of report cards. One by one, Mrs. Standish called out each person's name. We walked to the front of the room, shook Mrs. Standish's hand, and received our report card. Once we returned to our seat, everyone did the same thing—flipped the card over to see if they passed.

I was excited to see I had. You never know until you see the words:

Next Year's Placement Grade 6
Homeroom: Mrs. Jeffries
Room 346 Bradley Middle School

"Amy, I passed and I'm in Mrs. Jeffries' homeroom next fall. Whose room are you in?" I whispered over the calling of the bus numbers.

"Mrs. Jeffries? You are so lucky. I heard she's nice. I'm in Mr. Gordon's room. Oh no, that means we won't be together."

"We've been in the same room since first grade. I can't believe it. That stinks," I groaned.

"I know," Amy sighed. "And I never had a man for a teacher before."

"Oh, ya know what? I met this girl named Becky. She's in sixth grade right now and has Mr. Gordon. She told me he's really into science projects."

"Really? That's good."

"So you see, things might be better than you think."

Outside everyone said good-bye as they got on their different buses. It was weird to think we wouldn't be returning to Madison in the fall. I was excited about getting older, but also a little scared.

Amy and I sat down in the seat behind the driver. We started making plans for tomorrow's party.

"Shelly, I'm glad tomorrow's your party. We both need something to cheer us up. You know, not being in the same room and all."

I smiled and told her we would still be best friends.

Soon the bus pulled up to my stop. I said good-bye to my bus driver and ran off to my house. Mom was in the kitchen working on the favor bags for the party.

"Guess what?" I said as I put my backpack away. "I passed."

"Congratulations!" Mom said. She took the report card out of my hand and read it.

"See? I got an A+ on my oral report!"

"Yes, can't complain about that. Excellent job!"

"Mrs. Standish told me I gave one of the better reports. She said she could tell I prepared for it."

"Always shows. This is a wonderful report card, Shelly. I'm proud of you. You've worked hard. Oh, I see you have Mrs. Jeffries for your homeroom teacher next year? Are you happy about that?"

"Yeah, but Amy's in another room. That stinks."

"Those things happen, you know. You two can still be good friends."

"That's what I told her."

Mom put the box of neatly assembled favors on the dining room table. She stopped and admired them for a moment and then said, "I believe we're ready for the big party tomorrow."

I looked at the favor bags and mentioned how nice everything looked.

"Tomorrow's going to be fun!"

And with that said, I went upstairs to change into summer.

Chapter Eighteen
An Olympic Celebration

The first day of summer vacation is the best! It's freedom—two months of swimming, biking, reading, sleeping until eight, and just plain goofing off. Plus having an Olympic birthday party? Perfect.

I woke up to a sunny day with not a cloud in the sky. Dad opened the pool two weeks ago, so everyone came with their bathing suit. Several tables were set up on the patio for our lunch. Together, Dad and I planned pool games and races leading toward some friendly competition for the most medals—a regular Olympic celebration.

So that morning I quickly threw on my clothes and ran downstairs for breakfast. My mother was on the phone.

"No, Barb, I won't be able to make the first session. Shelly has a bunch of kids coming over for her birthday party this afternoon. I'll be at the next class though. Thanks for the reminder. Bye."

"Who was that?" Dad asked over his morning newspaper.

"That was Barb Fletcher. My quilting class starts today. I signed up but won't be making the first class."

"Quilting class?" I asked as I sat down at the table.

"Well, here's the birthday girl," Dad teased with a smile on his face. "How old are you now?"

"Eleven," I answered. Dad always asks me that on my birthday—as if he didn't know.

"Are you making a quilt?" I asked Mom.

"Yeah, it's a 100 Good Wishes Quilt for Mei."

"What's that?" I asked.

"There's a tradition in China. When a new baby is born, the family puts together a 100 Good Wishes Quilt for the child. It's called Bai Jia Bei. I'll tell you more about it later. Mrs. Fletcher is going to help me with it. Do you think you might want to come?"

"Maybe," I said as I checked out the two presents sitting on the counter.

"No opening those until after we have our family dinner tonight," Mom warned.

"Aaah—not fair."

"Your friends will be here soon so you better eat your breakfast and start setting up the games with your dad."

The time between breakfast and the first doorbell went by quickly. We had so many last minute preparations to do. Kaitlyn, this girl in my room, was the first to arrive.

"Hi, Kaitlyn. Come on in."

"Happy birthday, Shelly!" Kaitlyn handed me a present wrapped in white paper and decorated with large yellow sunflowers.

"What a pretty package. I love sunflowers! Thank you."

And so it went—one doorbell after another. I invited Kaitlyn and Erin from my class. Next, Natalie and Chelsea from our Chinese family support group arrived. I also decided to invite my new friend, Becky, whom I met during the Chinese language lessons. We had a lot in common, and I thought we could become good friends. Shortly after, Aunt Carol dropped Stephanie off at the house, and Amy was the last one to arrive. I opened the door and saw Amy standing there with this huge package in her arms. When I was small, my grandma warned me to not be so taken with large presents.

"Lots of wonderful gifts come in little boxes," she would tell me. But, I can't help it. The big packages always receive my total attention.

We went out to the pool and got into the fun of a party. Water was flying everywhere as each of us tried at making the biggest cannonball splash.

Dad, the judge, announced, "The award goes to Erin." We cheered as she accepted her medal.

Next was the relay race. We had two teams of four. One person from each team jumped into the water, swam down to the other end, and handed off a plastic ring to the next person waiting to swim back to the other side. The two teams went back and forth until each person had a turn. Our cheers of encouragement could be heard throughout my neighborhood. Water spilled over the sides of the pool as each girl tried to out swim the other.

Dad yelled, "Team Two wins the race! Erin, Natalie, Stephanie, and Shelly—come up for your medals." With a sense of pageantry, Mom hung a medal around everyone's neck. Erin beamed as she looked down at the two medals she now wore.

For the third event, we competed to see who could stand on her hands the longest. Four of us tried at one time. Then the next four did it. Finally, the winner of the first group went up against the winner of the second group.

Becky was the holder of the medal this time.

And so the afternoon went. There were back stroke races; a contest to capture the most rings at the bottom of the pool; and the funniest dive competition. The afternoon was filled with games, eating, and lots of giggles.

Before we had cake, I opened all the colorful packages piled on the back porch table. I purposely saved Amy's large package for last. As I carefully pulled at the paper, I wondered what it could be.

"Another wrapped package?" I asked. Amy smiled and said, "Open it."

When I did I found a third wrapped package inside.

"Open it!" the girls screamed.

Before long I was holding another wrapped gift. Everyone started laughing. This continued several more times until I finally held a small white box in my hands. My very large present actually shrunk before my eyes.

"Open it, open it!" the girls demanded.

"Is it going to be another wrapped box?" I asked Amy.

"I don't know. Look and see," she answered. Slowly, I unwrapped it and found a shiny white box with cut flowers on the top.

"I love it!" I said. Everyone crowded around to see my gift. "Look! It has these beautiful purple flowers on it."

"Those are plum blossoms. Didn't you say Mei's name means plum blossom in English?"

"It does. That is so cool."

"My mom helped me pick it out," Amy said. "We went into this jewelry store to get it. The lady there said the box was made out of porcelain."

"Yeah, it feels like the porcelain doll I have."

"She told us porcelain was first made in China. For the longest time they wouldn't tell anyone how they made it."

"Really? This is so pretty. Xie xie, Amy."

"Xie xie?"

"That means 'thank you' in Chinese," Becky answered feeling quite smart.

"How do you say 'you're welcome'?" Amy asked.

"By yong xie," Becky and I said together. The girls started mimicking "xie xie" and "by yong xie".

"Looks like the Chinese lessons are paying off for the two of you girls," Dad said to us. We giggled as we listened to the girls trying to speak Chinese.

Like all fun times, they come to an end. So it was for my Olympic birthday party. I picked up around the pool area and took all my gifts to my room. Later that evening, we had our family dinner and I opened the two gifts from my parents. I received two sets of shorts and tops.

"Thank you, I really needed some summer clothes."

"You're welcome. Oh, we almost forgot. We have something else for you," Dad teased as he got up from his chair. He picked up this long string and handed it to me.

"What's this? A string?"

"Uh huh, why don't you see where it takes you?" Dad suggested.

I followed the string into the dining room, the kitchen, and the hallway. Before I knew it, there was a scrambled heap of string in my hands.

"When does this stop?" I laughed. "I had to work for Amy's gift and now this?"

"Just keep going!" Mom advised.

The string took me toward the mudroom where the washer and dryer stood.

"Nothing here; the string keeps going." Eventually the string led to the garage door. Mom and Dad were right behind me when I opened the door. There in the garage stood a blue mountain bike with big tires, a black seat, and shiny chrome. It even had a speedometer.

"Oh, WOW—a bike! It's beautiful! I can't believe it!" I yelled as I jumped up and down. I hugged my dad, then my mom, and then back to my dad again. "I didn't know I was getting a new bike!"

"You don't know everything," Mom laughed. "We felt you outgrew your old one. You've had it since you were six."

"Happy Birthday!" both Mom and Dad yelled.

No fooling! My first day being eleven? Perfect.

Chapter Nineteen
Bai Jia Bei

Summer vacation was one week old when Mom and I jumped into the car to attend Mrs. Fletcher's quilting class. It was held in a craft store downtown. I decided to tag along because there was absolutely nothing else to do. Amy left yesterday for a vacation at the beach. Erin was busy packing for a plane trip to Arizona to see her grandparents. And Stephanie was away at summer camp for a week. After such a fun start to summer, it was beginning to look like a boring week.

"So what's this bah gee whatever quilt you're making?" I asked half interested as we drove to the class. Boy, did I regret this decision to go! Boring, boring, boring!

Mom laughed. "I think you mean Bai Jia Bei. It means a blanket united by 100 families."

"One hundred families? Why's the quilt named that?" I asked.

"Well, the custom is to ask 100 friends and family to

send a patch of cloth with a note of good luck for the baby," Mom said.

"Sweet—but what do you do with all of the stuff once you get it?"

"That's where the blanket comes in. You know how a quilt is made up of different pieces of material? After we receive each fabric, we cut out a large square of the material and sew it into the quilt. Then a smaller piece of the cloth goes into a creative memory book along with the wish for the child."

"Why do all that?" I yawned as I watched the trees whiz by the car window. No doubt about it—a boring day.

Mom looked over at me and smiled. "When Mei is older, she can select a patch on the finished quilt and find its matched pair in her memory book. Then she can see who gave it to her, and read the wish they had for her when she became a member of our family."

"That's kinda cool. Do you have all 100 patches?"

"I'm getting there. I wrote letters and sent emails to people we know, telling them about the adoption, and asking if they would like to participate. So far I've received about 85 of the patches."

"Can you begin the quilt without all hundred?"

"I think so. I'll have ten squares going across and ten going down. Mrs. Fletcher's getting me started on it today."

"Are the squares with you?" I asked.

"Yeah, they're in those four large yellow envelopes on the backseat. You can look at a couple of them. Just don't mix them up. I have each square in a separate smaller envelope along with its wish."

I reached for an envelope and looked inside.

"These three are from Grandma, the Hoffmans, and the Presleys. Did you ask Amy's family to do this, too?"

"I did. They said they'll get it all together after they

return from their vacation."

"Look at this one! It has ladybugs on it."

"I'm not surprised," Mom said as she glanced over at the patch I held up to the light. "Did you know ladybugs stand for good luck? If you see a ladybug, good things will happen."

"Yeah, I like ladybugs. They're the only insect I like— except for dragonflies and butterflies. I think they're pretty, too." For some strange reason, I found myself getting interested in this quilting project. "Can I do a square?"

"Of course, that's an excellent idea," Mom said. We'll look for material at the fabric shop before we leave."

"I don't want to give Mei just any old fabric. I want it to be special."

"Sure. You can pick out something you like," Mom said.

"No, I have a better idea. Remember my old blankie that helped me fall asleep at night?"

"How could I forget that thing. For the longest time, you wouldn't go to sleep without it. I remember the day you decided you no longer needed it. You were four years old. We had a big celebration as you gently put it in the box. Do you remember doing that?"

"Ah huh, I felt sad I wouldn't be using it anymore, but I knew I had to stop. Still, I wasn't ready to throw it away."

Mom smiled and said, "I think it's on the top shelf of my closet. Are you thinking of using part of that blanket for your square?"

"Yeah, do you think I should?"

"Definitely! That's a clever idea. I'll get it down and give it a good washing. Then you can cut two squares from the part that's still in good shape. From what I remember, the edge of the blanket was in shreds."

"From too much hugging," I said as I reached over to

change the radio station.

Mom had this grin on her face as our car pulled into the parking lot. When we got inside the shop, I sat down and listened to Mrs. Fletcher give instructions on how to cut the fabric squares, and pin them onto the plum colored backing Mom purchased for the project. I couldn't wait to get home to contribute my square. It was good to know there would be another use for the blanket that comforted me when I was small. It made me feel safe. Maybe it will do the same for Mei.

"I still need to think about the wish. I want it to have some meaning," I told Mom after the class was over. "You know—not just good luck or welcome to the family."

"Just keep thinking about it. Something will pop into your head," Mom suggested.

As it turned out, I didn't have to wait too long. Later that evening, I remembered an old Chinese saying I saw in several of the books I used for my report at school. I mentioned it to Mom as I got ready for bed.

"Do you remember how the saying went?" Mom asked.

"Not exactly, but I think I can find it in my notes."

I looked through my papers until I found what I was looking for. "Look, here it is!" I held up the notebook and read the words.

"An invisible red thread connects those who are destined to meet, regardless of time, place, or circumstance. The thread may stretch or tangle, but will never break."

"I like that, Shelly. I really do. It fits!"

"The only thing," I said, "is the red thread is really meant to connect a girl with the guy she would someday marry."

"That's okay. We can twist the meaning around a little so that it fits us."

"Could we hang a red thread from the patch?"

"Sure, we'll braid some strands and then tack it onto your square," suggested Mom.

Later that night while I was in bed, I thought about my blanket and the red thread idea. How true that old Chinese saying is! There is an invisible thread connecting me to my little sister. We might have to wait awhile and there could be obstacles, but that thread won't break. We are destined to meet.

Chapter Twenty
Where's the Pizza?

"Hurry up, Shelly. We're going to be late," yelled Dad.

"I'll be right down," I called out as I struggled with the new charm bracelet Natalie and Chelsea gave me for my birthday. It had five Chinese symbols on it. One stood for love, the others for happiness, good luck, long life, and wealth. I wanted to wear it to the dinner the Boyds were having today. I finally got it clasped, ran downstairs and got into the car. It wasn't a long drive, and soon we were pulling up to the white house that sat on the corner of a quiet street.

"Looks like the Averys are here," Mom pointed out as she opened the car door. As soon as the car's motor shut off, Natalie appeared from around the side of the house.

"Hi, Shelly. Chelsea isn't here yet."

"Hi, Natalie. Look! I'm wearing my charm bracelet."

"Awesome. Come on; let's play volleyball in the

backyard. There's a net up."

It wasn't long before everyone arrived, and Chelsea and her brother, Jon, joined us in the backyard. We played several games before we were called in for dinner.

"Come in, kids. We're getting ready to eat," called Mrs. Boyd.

Each family brought food from a particular section of China, and displayed it on separate tables.

"I didn't know Chinese food could be so different," Chelsea whispered to me.

"Thanks so much for participating in this dinner," announced Mrs. Boyd. "Everything looks and smells so delicious. I thought before we eat, we should hear about the food. Who wants to start?"

"I will," said Mrs. Presley. "We brought Cantonese food."

"What's Cantonese?" asked four year old Kim Boyd.

"It's the kind of cooking from the Guangdon Province and Hong Kong," answered Mr. Presley.

"Where's that?" asked Kay Hoffman.

"We have some very curious children here," laughed Mrs. Presley. "Canton use to be the name of an old port city in southern China. Today that city is called Guangzhou. That's the area our Emily came from." Everybody looked over at Emily and smiled. Feeling a little shy, she giggled and hid her face in her hands.

"In this province you'll find steamed fish and roast suckling pig. Cantonese restaurants usually have live fish in tanks. When you go in to eat, you get to choose which fish you want. Then it's cooked for you and served with mild sauces," explained Mr. Presley.

"We don't have the fish tank here, but we do have some fish you can try," Mrs. Presley added.

I looked on the table and saw a large plate of fish with

several small bowls of sauce. I thought I might try some of that. I do like fish.

"Looks delicious," remarked Mrs. Hoffman. "We brought Mandarin Chinese. It's food from the area that was once called Peking, but is now known as Beijing. We flew into that city when we went to get Kay and Thomas. They use leafy cabbage and wheat instead of rice. What I put together for us are crepe wraps with pork inside."

"Why is there a pot of water on the table?" I asked.

"Oh, it's not just water. It's actually soup broth. The pot is here so you can cook your own meat and vegetables right at the table."

"Sounds like fun," Natalie said as she smelled the steam coming from the pot.

"Sue, where's the Peking duck?" laughed my dad.

"We left it hanging on a line at home," teased Mrs. Hoffman. Everyone laughed, but I didn't get what was so funny until my Mom explained how you see ducks hanging in the front windows of Chinese restaurants, especially in China Town.

"Can we eat now?" asked Natalie's sister, Lin.

"No, not yet," Mrs. Hoffman said. "Not everyone has talked about their food."

"What kind of Chinese food is this?" Lin asked as she pointed to another table.

"What's it called again, Mom?" asked Natalie.

Mrs. Avery walked over to her table. "This is called Sichuan. It comes from the Western part of China. They tend to use a lot of chili peppers, red peppercorns, ginger, and pickled vegetables. The food is very spicy. This part of China traded with India for centuries, and copied some of their cooking styles. This is Szechuan beef and stir fried green beans. These cold noodles are served with this peanut sauce here."

I wasn't too sure about this one. I'm not crazy about real spicy food. I looked up and saw Mom giving me her "just try it" look. I swear. Mothers can read minds. Very scary!

Soon we were in the living room looking at the food Mr. and Mrs. Boyd brought.

"Shrimp? This looks good," my dad announced as he took one off the plate. "Where's this type of cooking from, Dave?"

"It's from the Zhejiang Province which is in the southeastern part of China. It's actually called Shanghai cuisine. The people there do a lot of braising and stewing. They also use very rich sauces. We made this shrimp and wine chicken for everyone to try."

"I'm getting hungry just looking at this spread," said Mr. Avery.

"So what did your family bring, Shelly?" asked Jon.

I pointed to the table displaying the food my mom prepared.

"It's called Hunan," mentioned my mom.

"You want to be careful when you eat this because it's very hot and I don't mean the temperature," warned Dad.

Mom said, "We brought samples of stir fried chicken and spicy eggplant in garlic sauce."

After we heard about the different Chinese cooking (Hunan, Canton, Sichuan, Mandarin, and Shanghai), everyone took a plate and started sampling everything.

I walked around the five tables with my empty plate and set of chopsticks, and wondered what I would eat. I went up to Chelsea and Natalie and whispered, "Where's the pizza?"

My mom overheard me and quietly scolded, "Shelly, that's not polite. Besides, you better get used to this. You'll be eating Chinese food for two weeks."

Chapter Twenty One
Back to School

If I had to name a season that had wings, it would be summer. It flies right by. So if summer has wings, winter has concrete boots. Autumn is sandwiched somewhere in between. Who knows what happens to that season? Just after the trees lose their leaves, not too much time goes by before that freezing white stuff starts to fall. Actually, summer doesn't end until September 21. But for us kids? It ends on the first day of school.

The one good thing about starting a new school year is the back-to-school shopping. Between June and September, I grow. It's funny because I never noticed myself growing between October and January or between February and May. So why is it that I grow during the summer? Maybe it's the sunshine that does it.

Getting on the bus was not fun. I climbed the stairs, faced a new driver, and saw 20 faces staring at me as I took a seat at the front of the bus. I later discovered the 7th and 8th graders like to sit in the back of the bus.

"Hi, Shelly. Aren't you excited about going to the middle school?" Amy asked as she sat down next to me.

"It would be better if we were in the same homeroom," I answered. "It's scary enough being on this bus with all these bigger kids. I feel so little. What's it going to be like when we get to school?"

"I think 6th grade is going to be awesome," Amy answered as she tried to cheer me up. I envied Amy with all her self-confidence. I'm usually thinking about how things could go wrong. She never does that. So why do I?

We arrived at Bradley Middle School and left the security of the bus for unknown territory. I immediately noticed there were no kindergarten kids walking in with their name tags on. Instead, I saw these big 7th and 8th graders. Just like the ones on my bus. Next to them, I felt like a five year old—not knowing where I was going or what I was doing. All I needed was a "My name is SHELLY" tag.

The wide halls were lined with lockers with those dreadful combination locks. I heard the horror stories of 6th graders who couldn't figure out how to open their locker to get to their books. Will that happen to me? I would just die!

The floors sparkled and the walls were freshly painted. While we were on vacation, I could tell some people were in here working.

If anyone wanted to know what's in style, just check out kids on the first day of school. It's like a fashion show. The styles were new, but everyone was dressed the same. I'm not quite sure where I'll fit in.

"Shelly, Amy, wait up!" It was Erin. We were so

excited to see someone we knew.

"Erin, how was your trip out west?" I asked. Erin's family left early in the summer for a trip to Arizona to see her grandparents who moved there last November.

"Oh, it was fun, but awfully hot. We saw amazing things. They have these big reddish rocks all over the place. My dad called them sandstone formations. We even visited a Hopi reservation."

"What's that?" Amy asked.

"A reservation? You know, land set aside for the Native Americans. The Hopi is a tribe that lives out there in the desert. We actually stayed over night at a hotel that's part of the reservation. It was right on the mesa."

"Awesome. Did you see the Grand Canyon?" I asked. "I've seen pictures of it and always wanted to go there."

"We did. My grandfather drove us there from Phoenix. It was so huge. At first you don't see it. But then, as you get closer to the edge, you look over and see this giant hole in the ground. I wanted to hike down to the Colorado River, but it would take too long. We could have used mules, but my grandparents weren't interested in doing that at all. Did either of you go anywhere?"

"Yeah, I went to the ocean," said Erin. "We stayed in a condo right on the beach. It was so much fun. I even tried surfing."

"What about you, Shelly?"

"No, my dad's saving his vacation for China."

"That's right. What's happening with that?" asked Erin.

"We're still waiting for the referral. It shouldn't be too much longer."

"Are you still going to China with your parents?"

"Uh huh, but I'm kinda nervous. I heard we'll be on two planes to get there. And one of them is for thirteen hours straight."

"Whew! That's a long time to be on a plane," Amy said.

"Yeah, especially seeing I've never been on a plane in my life!"

"Oh, this looks like my room. Erin, which homeroom are you in?" asked Amy.

"Mrs. Donovan's—we're all in different homerooms. I don't have a clue who's in my class."

"Welcome to the club!" I said sarcastically. "Make sure you save me a seat at lunch."

Chapter Twenty Two
The Referral

I t contained a letter and a couple of pictures of a small child. The letter said she was dropped off at an orphanage in Chengdu when she was four weeks old. The three of us sat on the other side of the desk from Mrs. Cardona at the adoption agency. She called us into her office to talk about the newly arrived referral.

"The baby is 11 months old," said Mrs. Cardona.

We looked at the photos. One showed a very small child lying on a blanket with a bottle in her hand. The other picture showed her being held by one of the nurses. I stared at both of the pictures for the longest time.

"Mom, her face is perfectly round and her eyes are so bright and dark."

"I know! Look at the huge smile that's on her face." We loved her immediately.

"I want to go get her now," I said. Mom reached over and squeezed my hand. I think she felt the same way.

Mrs. Cardona smiled and said, "The first thing you need to do is decide if this is the child you want."

We looked at the photos and together said, "YES!"

"I can see there's no hesitation here," Mrs. Cardona laughed. "I'll let the CCAA know of your acceptance. You should be given your travel approval in probably three weeks."

"Does that mean we'll be going in three weeks?" I asked feeling all excited.

"Actually, Shelly, it's more like 6 weeks. You have to wait awhile after your approval to get all your travel arrangements made. Plus, you'll have to apply for a visa," Mrs. Cardona answered.

"What's a visa?" I asked Mrs. Cardona.

"It's a paper that allows you to travel for a limited amount of time in China. Without that paper and your passport, you can't get into the country."

"Boy, you need to have lots of patience when you're adopting a baby," I pointed out.

"You need to have lots of patience after you get the baby, too," Mrs. Cardona said as she winked and patted me on the arm.

"We're getting there," Dad reminded me.

"Speaking about getting there, I'm inviting all of you to a gathering at the adoption center where you can meet the other families in your traveling group."

"Oh, when's that?" Mom asked.

"Three weeks from tomorrow."

"Sounds good. We'll be there." Dad answered.

"Who are they?" I asked.

"They're the people who'll be traveling with us to pick up Mei," answered Mom.

"That's right," said Mrs. Cardona. "When parents travel to China to pick up their baby, they don't go alone. They're usually in a group. There will be five other families traveling with you to pick up their babies. Because you'll be spending so much time with them, we suggest you meet each other beforehand."

"Will the children be coming from the same orphanage?" Dad asked.

"Yes," Mrs. Cardona answered as she stood up and walked over to the door of her office.

"The girls will be like sisters," I said.

"Shelly, in a way you're right," Mrs. Cardona replied. "So, congratulations! We'll be waiting for your travel approval to arrive."

Chapter Twenty Three
Mid-Autumn Festival

"Welcome," Mom said to the Averys as they arrived at our house for the Mid-Autumn Festival.

"What a perfect evening!" Mrs. Avery said.

"Yes, we're lucky. The moon should be very full and large today. Let's go outside. Everyone is out there now."

Natalie and her little sister, Lin, came out the back door looking for me. "Shelly, do you know what this festival is about?"

"Not really. All I know is we're having a barbecue under the moon." I looked over and saw my dad cooking pork on the grill. Everyone else pitched in and brought salads and other side dishes. It looked delicious.

After we finished our meal, Mrs. Presley announced,

"We have some good news for you. Jeff and I completed adoption papers for another little girl from China. Emily will soon have a little sister."

Everyone was happy for them. I couldn't help but giggle to myself when I heard Mrs. Presley say the word, SOON. If there's something adoption isn't, it's soon.

"We're waiting for our home visit," Mr. Presley told us.

"That's so exciting. There's going to be two new babies added to our support family," Mrs. Hoffman pointed out.

"Have you noticed it's getting dark earlier now?" Mrs. Avery asked.

We looked up at the harvest moon that was now large and brilliant. Its presence seemed so close to Earth, I felt I could reach out and grab it.

"Before we tell you about the mid-autumn festival, we're going to serve fruit and moon cakes," said Mom.

"Moon cakes?" the group asked.

Everyone wanted to know what moon cakes were.

"They're flaky pastry stuffed with a filling," Mom said. "This festival is held in mid-autumn when the moon is large like it is tonight. The Chinese watch the moon while they drink wine, eat fruits, and moon cakes. Shelly, would you and Chelsea go and get them for us?"

We went into the kitchen looking for the cakes my mother made that afternoon.

"Here they are," I told Chelsea.

"They're so cute. What's inside?" Chelsea asked as she picked up one of the two trays.

"My mom told me that in China the cakes are sometimes stuffed with egg yolk, lotus seed paste, red bean paste, and coconut."

"Oh!"

I could see by the look on Chelsea's face this was something she wasn't interested in trying.

"But my mom stuffed them with walnuts and dates."

"Now that sounds better," Chelsea said as she gave a sigh of relief.

We brought the trays outside and placed them on the picnic table.

"What's this on the top of the cakes?" Jon asked.

Dad said, "Both of these are Chinese symbols. This one stands for harmony and peace. That one stands for a long life."

"Like my charm bracelet," I said holding my wrist over my head.

"That's right. You know, there's a beautiful story that goes along with all of this."

"Let's hear it," Mr. Boyd said as he put a moon cake on his plate.

"It seemed Hou Yi was a very mean ruler who won this potion that would allow him to live forever."

"What's a potion?" asked Kim.

"Oh, it's like a magical drink."

"How did he win it?" Lin wanted to know.

"Good question, Lin. By shooting nine suns out of the sky with his bow and arrow," Mom said.

"Is this pretend?" asked Kim.

"Yes, it's like a legend, Kim. You know, a story that's handed down from person to person," explained my dad.

"Just like you're telling us now," pointed out Emily.

"Right on! Anyways, getting back to the story, Hou Yi won this potion. His wife, Chang E, didn't want him to drink it. She feared if her husband did drink it, he would never die. That would mean the people's lives would be miserable forever."

"What did she do?" asked Natalie.

"She drank the potion. It made her very light, and she floated up into the moon. The Chinese like to think of the moon as Chang E's home."

"There's also another version to this story," Mom added. "Often the Chinese children are told there's a fairy that lives in a large but cold crystal palace on the moon. This fairy has no one there with her but one jade rabbit."

"A jade rabbit?" asked Chelsea.

"Hey, at least it's not a dragon," I teased.

"No dragons in this story," laughed Mom. "Well, once in awhile a heavenly general would visit her, and he'd bring a very good wine. The fairy would drink the wine and then dance. They say this explains the shadows on the moon's surface."

"I think this festival also symbolizes the coming together of family," Mr. Avery said.

"It's certainly bringing our support family together," said Mrs. Boyd.

Everyone looked up at the full moon that was lighting up the sky. We ate our moon cakes and listened to the songs of the insects. It didn't feel autumn, but we all knew it would be one of our last pleasant nights before it turned cold.

Chapter Twenty Four
Superstitions

Sixth grade at the middle school turned out to be a good thing. Even though Amy and Erin were not in my homeroom, I still liked being there. I actually made a new friend this year. Her name was Katie and she moved here from Boston.

Katie sat behind me in class which was how I got to know her. Both of us were a little lost that first day. I didn't know anyone in the room, but she didn't know anyone in the school. So we became friends.

In some ways we're alike. We both like to read mystery stories and watch the same TV shows. Neither of us enjoys long car rides, but we both like to play word games. The strangest thing, however, is that we're both superstitious.

I noticed Katie always wore this unicorn around her

neck. "Why do you wear that unicorn all the time?" I asked one day at lunch.

"Oh, the unicorn is a symbol for good luck. My cousin gave it to me for my birthday."

"Do you think it works?" I asked.

"Don't know, but I'm not taking any chances."

"I have a lucky stone," I confided. "Here it is. I always have it in my pocket. See how smooth it is. Sometimes people call it a worry stone, but I think of it as my lucky token."

"I like the way it feels. Where did you get it?"

"Last year we went to a museum and they had a bin of them. This is the one I picked out. Its brought me nothing but good luck."

Katie leaned over and whispered, "Promise you won't tell anyone?"

"I promise."

"Well, I can't sleep at night unless I have my closet door shut."

"Why's that?" I asked.

"I don't know. Just another superstition of mine. Do you have any others?"

"I do." I looked around to see if anybody was listening to our conversation. When the coast was clear, I said, "Whenever I take a test I wear the same pair of socks."

"No fooling. Do you have them on now?"

"No, we don't have any tests today."

"What do the socks do?" Katie asked looking amused.

"Probably nothing, they just give me confidence."

"What's going to happen when they fall apart or no longer fit?" Katie asked.

"I've already thought about that. I hope to break in another pair soon, but I'm nervous to do it. You know, what will happen if the new ones don't work?"

At that moment, Katie jumped up and said, "I have a solution! This is what you do. Wear one of your lucky socks and one brand new sock together. Do that for several tests. Then once that new sock is broken in, wear it with its match."

"Hmmmm, that's a good idea," I said. "I'll try it out next week for the math test. Math isn't hard for me."

We both started laughing because even though we were dead serious, we could also see the silliness of it all.

After school I told Mom about Katie and how we both are a little superstitious. I didn't mention anything about the socks.

"What makes people become superstitious, Mom?"

"I don't know, but it's been going on for centuries. Many people won't walk under a ladder. Other people get nervous if a black cat walks across their path, while some are afraid to come out on Friday the thirteenth."

"Are you superstitious?" I asked as I followed her into the family room.

"Not anymore, but I remember when I was little I wouldn't step on a crack in a sidewalk. Of course, no worries about that here. We don't have sidewalks!"

"Do you think the people in China are superstitious?" I asked.

"I wouldn't be surprised. Deep inside, people are the same all over the world."

When I asked what their superstitions might be, Mom suggested I look it up on the internet. After a little searching, I called to her.

"Mom, come here. Look."

"What? Anything about lucky socks?"

"How did you know about that?" I asked.

She laughed as she walked over, looked at the computer monitor and said, "Just a hunch!"

"But you never said anything." I felt like my secret was now out in the open.

"Well, neither did you," Mom answered.

We read what the website had to say about the superstitions of the Chinese when Mom said, "Looks like tigers' claws, old brass mirrors, and cords worn around the neck are all things that are used for both good luck and to scare away evil spirits."

"Yeah, and the number four is thought of as being bad luck in China. They never put four chairs at a table, and elevators never have a button with a four on it."

"That's similar to what we do but with the number 13," Mom said.

"I heard about buildings having a twelfth and fourteenth floor, but never a thirteenth."

We read more about the superstitions in China. For example, if you're at someone's house having tea, never point the spout of the teapot towards someone. That would be bad luck.

"Mom, did you know the Chinese people feel eclipses are due to a dragon trying to eat the sun or the moon? Isn't that weird?"

"The mind plays funny tricks on all of us, Shelly. It doesn't matter if you're American or Chinese."

Chapter Twenty Five
The Year of the Monkey

Happy Birthday, dear Grandma,
Happy Birthday to you!

And so we sang from the tops of our lungs as my grandmother blew out her candles. We were at Aunt Carol's house celebrating Grandma's birthday.

"How old are you, Grandma?" my cousin, Stephanie, asked?

"Not telling," is all Grandma said.

"We tell you our age," I reminded her.

"Well, there's this unwritten law that says you don't have to tell anyone how old you are once you pass forty. So it's a secret."

"Can't you just tell me?" Stephanie begged. "Come on, give us a hint."

"Okay, but only a hint. Our family has been into learning about China, so here's your clue. I was born in the Year of the Monkey."

Mom and Aunt Carol laughed as they saw confusion written across our faces.

"What's that about?" I asked Mom.

"It has to do with the Chinese lunar calendar. They believe each year has a different animal sign. They call these Chinese Zodiac signs."

Uncle Charlie added, "There are twelve of these signs and once you get to the twelfth sign, you start over with the first."

I wondered what my sign was as I took a bite of the birthday cake. I announced to the group my plan of looking it up on the internet when I got home.

"Look up Zodiac signs and see what it says for the year you were born," Uncle Charlie suggested.

"Yeah, and while you're at it, maybe you can figure out the year Grandma was born. You know her sign is the Year of the Monkey," my dad winked as he looked over at Grandma.

"Hey, leave me out of this!" Grandma warned.

When we returned home from the party, I immediately sat down in front of the computer and typed in Zodiac signs.

My dad walked over to see what I was doing. "I knew it wouldn't be long before you started looking for your sign."

"Look, here's a bunch of numbers. Are these the years?" I asked.

"Ah huh, just click onto the year you were born and see what it says."

"I was born in the Year of the Ox."

"Okay, now let's see what that means. Here! It says you're a born leader and very confident."

"Who came up with all of this?" I asked.

"I don't know. Check out if there's any history about it.

Oh, look! This might help us out," Dad said as he pointed to another link.

I clicked onto that link, and a short explanation popped up before us.

"Listen to this," I said. "Chinese legend says that Buddha gave a call for all of the animals to come to him. Those who came had a year named for them. So these must be the animals that came."

"What do we have here?" That's what my dad says when he's trying to figure something out. "There's the rat, the ox, tiger, rabbit, dragon."

"I'm not surprised to hear there's a dragon. There's always a dragon!" I said.

"You're right," Dad agreed. "There's always a dragon hanging around somewhere. After the dragon, there's a snake, horse, sheep, monkey."

"MONKEY!" I yelled. That's the year Grandma said she was born. I think I can figure this out," I mentioned with the confidence only an ox would have.

"Your grandmother's not going to like what you're doing here," Dad warned me.

"She gave the clue," I reminded him. "Now if all of the monkeys happen every twelve years…hmm…it says 2004 was the last Year of the Monkey. So that must mean the other years that had the same sign would be 1992, 1980, 1968, and 1956. Was she born in 1956?" I asked.

"Would that make sense?" Dad asked as he went into the kitchen to get his reading glasses.

"I don't know."

"Think about how old your mom is," Dad yelled from the kitchen.

"Oh, yeah. No, that would make Grandma too young. I

think I need to go back another twelve years. When I do that, then the year she was born would be 1944. Now that makes sense. Because if I go down to 1932, that would make her older than I know she is! Grandma was born in 1944. We did it!"

"No, no! Don't include me. You're the one who figured it out," Dad said as he chuckled to himself.

"Wait until I tell Stephanie," I said.

"Do you think that would be a nice thing to do?" Mom asked as she walked into the room and gave my dad an annoyed look. "You know, Shelly, you need to consider other people's feelings. Age and weight can be a little touchy with some people. If your grandmother doesn't want to announce her age, you need to respect that."

"So I shouldn't tell anyone?"

"What's the little voice inside you saying right now?" Mom asked.

Whenever Mom brings up the little voice inside me, I always know what the answer is. And most of the time I don't like the answer.

"Okay. It's saying to keep my mouth shut."

"So," Mom replied, "maybe that's exactly what you should do!" And that's exactly what I've done. Grandma's age is safe with me.

Chapter Twenty
Six
Getting It All Together

"**W**e're leaving in three weeks!" I told Amy on the phone. We received the approval this afternoon."

"That is sooo cool!"

Amy always says that whenever she thinks something good is happening.

"Yeah, we have our passports, visas, airplane tickets, and itinerary."

"It's going to happen for you, Shelly."

"Yup, we just need to finish packing. One of the suitcases is for Mei. My mom's packing disposable diapers, and enough clothing to last 10 days."

"I can't wait to see the baby," said Amy. "You're going to have an awesome trip. Wish I could go."

"Wouldn't that be the best…if you could?"

"Shelly, I need you up here," Mom called from the bedroom.

"Oh, I better go, Amy. See you on the bus, tomorrow."

"Okay, bye."

I went upstairs and found my mom still packing Mei's bag.

"Watcha doin'?" I asked.

"Oh, I have some things here for Mei—a couple of small blankets, a diaper bag, small packages of cereal, applesauce, things like that."

"Are you taking these toys?"

"I thought I would pack them for the long plane ride home."

Mom opened up another suitcase. "Shelly, would you go to your room and get that pile of clothes I've stacked on your bed?"

"Sure." I left, got the pile, and brought it back to the room.

"Thanks. Just put it next to the suitcase."

Dad came in and picked up the packed suitcase and placed it in the corner of the room. "I think we'll leave the luggage over here until we take off next week."

"This is about all I can do for now," said Mom. "Whatever else we need can be packed just before we leave. We're going to be so busy next week. It's good we're taking care of this now."

Dad looked over at me as I sat on the edge of the bed. "Shelly, one thing you should know is after we get Mei, she might have some adjustment problems. She won't be familiar with our house, our ways of doing things, or us."

"I know. Natalie told me when they picked up Kim, she didn't want to walk and they had trouble getting her to try."

"Mrs. Avery told me about that, too," Mom said. "They

also had a problem getting her to take a bath. She'd scream whenever they tried to give her one. We could experience some of that, too."

I looked over at the empty crib and said, "Yeah, she probably won't even know what we're saying. Right?"

"That's why we took a few Chinese lessons. Maybe knowing a few words will help us a little," Dad answered.

"Mom, Mrs. Jeffries wanted to know when we're leaving. I told her next week."

"Oh, that's right. I need to go and see her about the work you'll be missing while we're away."

"She said she mentioned it to all my teachers, and they'll put together the work before I leave."

"Super! It's a good idea to do as much as you can on the plane, Shelly. You'll have time on the long flight over but very little afterwards."

"Mrs. Jeffries said she's more concerned I keep up with math. Oh, and Mrs. Saunders, my Language Arts teacher, thought in place of doing the work I'd be missing, I could keep a detailed journal about my experiences."

"Great idea," said Mom. "Then we can include it in Mei's Lifebook."

"What worked out well is we'll be gone over Thanksgiving vacation so you won't be missing as many school days as we first thought," Dad said as he put a second suitcase in the corner.

"Our family will certainly remember this Thanksgiving Day," Mom said with a smile on her face. "We definitely have a lot to be thankful for."

Chapter Twenty
Seven
Off We Go!

"The taxi is here. Let's go!" yelled Dad from the living room. I hurriedly grabbed my backpack and ran downstairs. Mom took a last look around the house to make sure everything was okay, and then we hopped into the cab for that trip to the airport.

"How long will we be on the plane?" I asked.

"Well, we first fly to Chicago and that takes about 2 hours. Then we wait at Chicago's O'Hare airport for a few hours before we can get onto the plane that takes us to Beijing."

"Can the plane fly that far without stopping?"

"Sure."

"How long does it take to get to Beijing?"

"Close to 14 hours of flying time," Mom answered.

I looked out and saw the cold rain coming down on the front window. The windshield wipers made a soothing noise as they clicked back and forth, back and forth.

"When do we get to Beijing?" I asked.

Dad pulled out the paper with all the flight information on it. After studying it for some time he said, "It'll be 3:30 Thursday afternoon Beijing time. But it'll be 3:30 Thursday morning according to our clock. Beijing is 12 hours ahead of us in time."

Mom said, "It's going to be a long flight. That's why it's good you're wearing something comfortable."

"Dad, are we going to be on the plane all night?"

"You bet—all day and all night."

"How do we sleep?"

"The seats in the plane go back a little. You just try to sleep the best you can," Dad said.

When we arrived at the airport, we saw the other five families who were traveling with us. We met them a few weeks ago at the get together Mrs. Cardona arranged. Even though we didn't know each other, it didn't take long for everyone to get acquainted. Mom told me that happened when people have a lot in common.

Seated at the departure gate were the Tolsons, Knapps, Paynes, Muellers, and Humphreys. The Knapps were the only ones who were adopting a second child from China. This was a new experience for everyone else. They waved to us as we walked over to where they were sitting.

"So how's everyone doing?" my dad asked.

"A little tired, a little nervous, and very excited," Mrs. Tolson said. "Hi, Shelly, are you looking forward to your big adventure?"

"Shelly had a little trouble sleeping last night because it's her first time on a plane," Mom explained.

"First time? And it's to China!" Mrs. Tolson said.

"Don't worry, Shelly," Mrs. Humphrey reassured me. "Planes take off and land every minute of every day. Nothing to worry about. Justin and Andrea wish they could come, especially after they heard you were going."

Justin and Andrea are Mrs. Humphrey's kids. They're twins and a year younger than me. I was disappointed when I heard they wouldn't be going. I guess I'm lucky my parents are taking me. Everybody else's kids are staying home with someone.

I sat down in the empty seat next to Mr. Mueller, and opened up the new backpack my parents gave me last night. Inside they had little surprises like activity books, crossword puzzles, a mystery story, markers, colored pencils, and even a new video game. Of course, I also had to pack my math and science books and my journal from school. I pulled out the journal and opened to the first page.

"Writing in your journal?" Dad asked.

"Yeah, I thought I would write about how the trip started."

"Full of excitement?" said Mr. Mueller.

"For sure."

After getting down only a few thoughts, I heard the announcement that the plane to Chicago would be boarding shortly. I quickly put my journal back in my pack and we lined up to board.

"Mom, the plane is so large inside!" I saw rows of three seats on each side of the plane with a narrow aisle in between. The flight attendant looked at our tickets and pointed to our seats which were right over the wing. I took my place next to the window and clasped my seatbelt. After I settled in, I looked out the window. What I saw looked like an army of ants all doing their own special jobs. There were people loading the luggage onto the conveyor belt leading into the belly of the plane. Others were fueling the air craft, checking things under the wings, and driving little trucks from one plane to another.

"What's that guy doing?" I asked my mom.

Mom looked out the window and said, "Do you mean the guy with the baton in his hand? He helps the pilot taxi out onto the runway."

Shortly after she said that, we started to back up and get in line behind the other planes. While we sat on the runway waiting for takeoff, the flight attendant gave us instructions about what to do in case of an emergency.

Mom squeezed my hand and said, "We'll be up in the air before you know it. I heard the engines get louder and we started to move.

"We're in the air!" I said pointing to the roof tops and miniature sized cars below us. "You're right, Mom. It doesn't take long once we get moving."

After two hours of flying, we got off the plane in Chicago. We had plenty of time to get to Terminal 5 for our flight to Beijing. The whole group stayed together as we took the shuttle to that section of the airport.

When we arrived at our departure gate, Mrs. Payne asked, "So how did you enjoy your first plane ride, Shelly?"

"It wasn't bad," I answered. "I thought it would be bumpy like an amusement park ride, but instead it felt like we weren't even moving."

"It was a smooth flight," Mrs. Payne answered.

The second plane was much larger than the first one. In addition to the seats on the side, I saw a whole middle section of six seats across.

"Mom, I'm glad we're sitting by the window again."

We started to hear the familiar sound of the jet's engines. Mom leaned over and said, "The next time we're on the ground, we'll be in Beijing."

I nodded and sat back in my seat. I looked out the window and watched the land quickly disappear. With backpack in tow, I was ready for the long plane ride and the new adventure that was waiting for us in China.

Chapter Twenty Eight
Beijing

"This city was laid out according to feng shui principles," our guide told us while we rode in the small bus through the streets of Beijing.

"Dad, I remember reading about that feng shui stuff when I did my report in fifth grade. I didn't understand it though."

"I'll explain it to you when we get to the hotel. Right now, just look out the window and listen to what the guide has to say."

Why is it that grownups never want to explain things at the time we want an answer? But when we don't care to know, they go into nonstop talking.

The bus pulled over to let us off. We stood in front of a huge open area with lots of people walking around. John, our guide, called this place Tiananmen Square. In the center of this square stood a fountain that sent up several sprays of water with the largest one in the middle. At one end of the square I spotted a large government building with many columns.

John said, "This is Chairman Mao Memorial Hall. Chairman Mao was the leader who founded the People's Republic government of China back in 1949. He's buried in this building."

"Is that him?" I asked pointing to a very large picture of a man hanging down the front of another building.

"It is," John answered.

"Why do they have his picture hanging there if he's dead?"

"He's an important person to the Chinese people," John answered. "I think Americans do that. Don't you have many pictures and statues of George Washington in your country?"

"We do," I said as I nodded my head up and down.

John walked us to another part of the square and asked, "Does anyone know what that is over there?" He pointed to a tall stone monument.

"Looks like an obelisk," Mr. Payne answered. Mr. Payne was one of the people in our group. I watched him take one picture after another of almost every building we looked at. My parents also took lots of pictures, but Mr. Payne seemed to be a little out of control.

"What's an obelisk?" I whispered to my mom.

"It's a pillar with a pyramid shape on the top," she said.

Dad quietly added, "It's actually a pillar that has four sides to it, not a rounded one. Hey, you just had your math lesson for the day."

"Math?" I asked.

"Yeah, you know, geometry—Math."

John told the group that this obelisk was a monument honoring the people who died in the Communist Revolution.

Before we left for the trip, Mom bought me a camera to take my own photos. I decided to take a few pictures of the children flying kites in the square. I thought that would be more interesting than a building or a statue. Besides, Dad and Mr. Payne seemed to have them covered.

Many people kept coming up to us trying to sell us things.

"Hello, would you like to buy a baseball cap?"

"No, thank you," Dad politely answered.

"A book? Maybe a postcard? This nice T-shirt?"

Mom said she didn't want anything. But they kept following us around, lowering the price every time someone said no.

At first I thought things were very expensive, but soon learned that when I heard the cost of something being 22 juans, it was only three dollars. Mom finally broke down and bought a package of 10 postcards for 15 juans, or about two dollars. As soon as these vendors saw that, they swarmed over to us and tried even harder to sell their stuff.

John told us these people were known as the hello people because they always greeted tourists with their hellos.

Next we went to the Forbidden City. As we walked through each gate, all I could think about was the birthday present Amy gave me. It was the gift that had me opening up a large box only to find another box, and another, then another. That's what happened as we walked through the Forbidden City. We went through one gate into an open courtyard; to find a second gate that led to another courtyard; then a third gate...

"Is this all we're going to see?" I asked Dad. It was very windy and cold so I put on my heavier coat.

"There are six gates we have to walk through until we get to the emperor's palace," Dad mentioned as the wind blew dust into my eyes.

"Why was it built like this? There're no trees or grass or anything in these courtyards. It looks so bare."

"The emperor wanted it to be that way. He didn't want there to be places for his enemies to hide."

"I wonder why this is called the Forbidden City?"

John heard my question and answered, "It was forbidden for commoners to come inside the gate. They kept it that way for nearly 500 years."

"Look! I see two lions over there," I said as I pointed to two large statues.

"Oh yes, those are the bronze lions in front of the Hall of Supreme Harmony. Can you find something different between them?" John asked.

"No, they look alike," I said.

"Look again. Do you see the lion on the right? He has a large ball under his paw. That ball represents the earth and shows the lion's power. He's the male lion."

"Oh, yeah," said Mr. Humphrey. "The one on the left has a lion cub under her paw."

"She does. She's the mother lion," John told us as Mr. Payne took four more pictures.

"Now I think inside this building is the Dragon's Throne," Mrs. Tolson said as she looked at her Beijing tour book.

"It is," John said. "The last emperor was only three years old when he came into power. Because he was so young, his mother made decisions for him. As a young boy, he would sit on his throne. Directly behind him was a curtain that his mother would hide behind. She whispered the words he should say to the people that were visiting him."

Dad added, "I heard the young emperor's mother secretly ruled China throughout those years."

"That's right," John said. "She became known as the dragon."

We walked along the long narrow building looking into the windows. We could not go inside. I saw the throne and the curtain behind it. It was so dark and heavy inside the rooms.

"I would not have liked living here," I whispered to Mom. In the back of the emperor's palace was a garden of rocks and trees.

"This is where the young emperor played and later just sat and meditated until he was around 19," John continued to tell our group. "Then he was forced to leave the country."

After our day of exploring, we headed back to the hotel. It felt good to take a shower and get comfortable in my pajamas. But when I jumped on the bed, there was no bounce. We soon learned that Chinese people enjoy sleeping on hard beds.

"Can you tell me now?" I asked my dad. "You know, about feng shui?"

"I'm going for a shower. Your mom can tell you."

Mom sat down on the bed beside me. "You're right. These beds are hard."

"Told you so!"

Mom poked me in the ribs with her finger and I wiggled because it was my ticklish spot.

"Well, first of all, you are saying it wrong. Feng shui sounds like 'fung shwee.' It's an ancient Chinese practice that if you arrange objects correctly with space you will create harmony with the environment. Feng means wind and shui means water."

"How do you do that?" I asked.

"Think about how nice it is to go for a hike. You look up at the mountains. You see large trees and fields of flowers growing around you. There might even be a creek rushing by, and you feel like you're in harmony with the world. Everything flows and that is the type of environment feng shui tries to create inside your home."

"But what happens if you live in a place without mountains?" I asked. "What do you do then?"

Mom said, "Not a problem. Out in a small yard can be placed a mound of rocks which could represent the mountains. Plus there could be plants with perhaps a small fish pond. All of this creates that harmony."

I thought about that for a second and then asked, "Back at home I've seen these little dishes of rocks and water. Could that be used?"

"Definitely," Mom answered. "It doesn't take much to create that harmony. Water, plants, a mirror to reflect light, and the correct placement of furniture all are part of feng shui."

"China is really an interesting country," I yawned.

"It sure is. Now try to get some sleep. Tomorrow we fly to Chengdu."

Chapter Twenty Nine
My Sister, Mei

"Chengdu is known as the City of Hibiscus," John pointed out as we walked around the neighborhood near our hotel. "Chang Meng, an emperor in the tenth century, ordered the hibiscus be planted around the city walls. After all those years, the city still kept up the tradition."

I looked up at the buildings around us only to see them totally surrounded by mist. John told us the humidity is high here even when it's not hot. Along the sidewalks were planted ginko trees. These shaded the streets as we slowly walked along in the direction of the city's bonsai and flower market.

"This is a great place to shop for Sichuan handicrafts," John said.

"What's Sichuan?" I asked.

"It's one of the provinces of China, Shelly. Your country has states. China has provinces."

"Oh, I get it. In school we learned Canada has provinces, too."

"That's right, they do. Chengdu is a city in the Sichuan province. Matter of fact, this province has about ten percent of all of China's population."

We had to watch where we walked because the sidewalks were uneven and rough. But they weren't dirty. There was always someone with a funny looking broom sweeping them clean.

Soon we stumbled upon the market place and found a shop that made chops. These were stamps people used to sign their name on different documents.

"If you look closely," John pointed out, "all Chinese paintings have the artist's chop on it."

We decided to buy a chop for Mei. Mom picked out a smooth rectangular one that was made out of stone. It had a dog on the top because Mei was born in the year of the dog. She handed it to the man who sat in front of the shop. They bargained back and forth over a price until one was settled on. Finally, he started sanding the bottom of the chop until it was smooth. Then he carved out Mei's name in both Chinese and English.

"Dad, how does he get all those letters on the bottom of the chop?" I asked. "It's so small."

"I was thinking the same thing," admitted Dad. "Plus he has to carve everything backwards so it'll come out right when you stamp it on paper." We all watched with curiosity until everyone in the group had their own chop for their new daughter.

As we got ready to leave, I noticed a few people standing in front of the shop staring. "Why are they looking at us?" I asked.

"They're curious about you," John told me. "They don't get to see too many Western people here. In China it's not considered rude to stare at people. So just smile and say, 'Ni hau' (Nee How)."

"I know. That means hello."

Soon we stopped at a department store where everyone decided to get some things for the babies. Mom bought a few more clothes for Mei, plus she picked up a stroller. She decided to buy the stroller over here instead of getting it at home and lugging it on the plane.

"Besides," kidded Mom, "it's probably made in China, anyway!"

"We better pick up bottled water as we can't drink the water out of the hotel's tap," Dad added. "We'll also need it to brush our teeth."

Mom had a washcloth over the faucet as a way to remind us not to put our toothbrushes under the water. Taking a shower was also hard. I had to keep my mouth closed so water wouldn't get in. Keeping my mouth closed is not always easy!

On the way back to the hotel, we stopped to eat at a restaurant. Our group took up two tables. In the center of each table was a smaller turn table. At different times, several waitresses would put down dishes of food for us to share.

"You need to be careful when you spin the little table, Shelly," Mom warned as I eyed a dish of tomatoes at the opposite side of the turn table. "Someone may be helping themselves to something at their end."

Most of the food was really good, but some things were spicy and hot. Dad told me I should try a little of everything. What was weird is that near the end of the meal came the soup and rice.

"Wouldn't you think the soup and rice would come first?" mentioned Mrs. Payne.

"I know," answered Mrs. Mueller. "I like to put the vegetables and meat on top of my rice. We have to eat the rice plain when they serve it last."

The group figured out how to tell when the meal was over. It's when the plate of watermelon appeared.

"Do we get a fortune cookie?" I asked.

"No," answered John. "Not in China. Just in America. The meal usually ends in fruit."

When we finished eating, we hurried back to the hotel. The nurses were coming with the babies at seven o'clock and it was already five-thirty. As we left the restaurant, I pointed out a Kentucky Fried Chicken place across the road. "Can we eat there tomorrow, Dad?"

"We'll see, Shelly. Remember, we need to be flexible."

Back at the hotel room there were two small beds and one cot. I slept on the cot that was set up by the window. A metal crib was placed between the two beds.

"It's really going to happen, Steve," my mom said as she straightened the crib blanket. She sat down on one of the beds. "Yikes, this bed is really hard. I wonder if we should order a couple more comforters. We could sleep on top of one to make the bed a little softer."

Dad turned on the television to pass the time away. Only one channel was in English. It was a news channel. There wasn't much to do so I wrote in my journal about the day. The phone suddenly rang and everyone jumped.

"Ni hau," said Dad. "They are? Okay, we'll be right there. Good-bye."

"Are they here, Steve?" Mom asked. The shakiness of her voice hinted at her nervousness.

"We're supposed to go to John's room now."

As we walked down the hall, doors opened as the other

people in our group joined us.

"I am so nervous," Mrs. Payne told my mother.

"I know. We all are."

We entered John's room and saw seven women standing there. Six held small toddlers. "Which one is Mei?" I thought to myself. The one woman not holding a child looked to be in charge. John told us she was the director of the Children's Welfare Institute.

After a few words, John started to call out names and one by one, each couple received their child. Finally, our name was called. Mom smiled as she reached out for Mei. She looked a little older than her picture, but I knew it was her. I recognized the round face and the dancing black eyes. She stared at me, but I didn't quite know what to do.

Finally Dad said, "Hi, Mei. I'm your new daddy and this is your big sister, Shelly."

For over a year I thought about this moment—what clever thing I would say; what fantastic gesture I would make. Instead I did nothing. I finally gave a short wave and Mei reached out and grabbed my finger. We smiled at each other and became sisters.

Chapter Thirty
Morning with the Pandas

I t was nine o'clock when we returned to our room with Mei. Mom and Dad had a chance to speak to the woman holding Mei. She told us in Chengdu many of the children scheduled to be adopted leave the orphanage for foster care homes. So Mei was living with this woman's family. The lady looked sad as she handed her over to us. I felt bad for her. Mom promised the woman we would take good care of Mei and give her lots of love.

Once we were in the hotel room, Mom changed her from Chinese clothes to a diaper and pajamas. Mei never cried, but stared from Dad to Mom to me. Mom gave her a bottle of milk and soon she fell asleep in the crib between the two beds.

Mei's crying woke us the following morning. We all jumped and rushed to the crib. She stopped crying and sat up in her small bed. Mei looked at us through large tears which made her eyes appear even bigger.

"Good morning, Mei. Nei hau," said Mom as she lifted her small body out of the metal crib. "Today we're going to have some fun. Everyone is going to the Panda Sanctuary. But first, we need to give you a bath and have something to eat." Mom talked to Mei like she understood her.

"Mom," I said, "She doesn't understand English."

"I know, but that's how she'll learn it. We need to continuously talk to her about everything."

Mei didn't enjoy her bath. Actually, she screamed all through it. It saddened me and I wished she would stop crying.

"What I've heard from other people who've adopted, this is not unusual," Mom explained. "The children get washed but do not take baths very often. Putting them in a tub of water is frightening to them. But she'll soon get used to it."

We met our group at nine o'clock for our trip to the Panda Sanctuary. Everyone showed up looking happy but a little tired. On the bus John told us that these outings will help build a bond between each baby and her family. The Panda Sanctuary seemed to be a perfect place to start. Our guide explained the best time to visit the pandas is in the morning. That is when they are the most active.

John said, "The place we'll visit has the largest number of pandas on display anywhere in the world. There are about 1600 pandas living in the wild in all of China. So they are on the critically endangered list."

"How did they get on this list?" Mr. Mueller asked.

"There are several reasons for this," John explained. "The pandas are finicky eaters. They'll eat apples and carrots, but mostly thrive on bamboo as their main food source. This bamboo that grows in central China was being cleared out by people for development. The government is taking steps to stop this destruction. Also, poachers are a problem."

"What are poachers?" I asked John as we turned onto a street that showed a large panda poster.

"They're people who kill an animal in order to sell its hide. Panda hides can sell for as much as $10,000 in Hong Kong and Japan."

"How is China trying to turn this problem around?" Mr. Payne inquired.

"Well, there's a ten year plan. They're trying to preserve these natural habitats from extinction. Sanctuaries, such as this one, help the pandas exist and give birth to babies. There's also an effort being made by other countries. China will lend out pandas to zoos with the agreement that after the babies reach a certain age, they are returned to China."

I looked up at my mom and said, "I heard about all this on TV at Amy's house."

"Is the place we're going to a large zoo?" Mrs. Payne asked.

"The sanctuary is not a zoo, but is made to copy the panda's real habitat in nature," John answered. "You'll see acres of space for the pandas to roam and thrive. No other animals will be housed there."

Once we arrived, Dad pulled out the stroller and put Mei on the seat. The path was winding and led uphill going through what looked like a tunnel of bamboo. Everywhere I looked, I saw forests of bamboo. We stopped at this large statue of a mother and baby panda. It was made out of shiny metal and showed the baby sitting with his mother. It looked like a large gold ball as it reflected the sun's light. Everyone stood in front as John snapped a group photo.

We walked several minutes before the path opened to an area housing older pandas. They were so comical and huge as they sat there staring at us.

"I never knew they were this large," I said.

Dad took a picture with his camera and then said, "These are called Giant Pandas. They're big alright, and they look so clumsy, don't they?"

After we watched two of them sitting against a log, we continued along the path.

John stopped at another area and said, "This is the panda kindergarten. It's where the little pandas go after they're old enough to leave their mothers."

"They're so cute," I said as I watched two of them lay on their backs chomping on plants. "Is that the bamboo they're eating?"

"Yeah," said John. "Most pandas eat forty pounds of bamboo a day, but their body uses only about 8 pounds. The rest leaves the body as waste."

John warned not to let their cuteness fool us. "They're very strong animals and could be potentially dangerous," he said.

I could tell Mei and the other little girls were enjoying the pandas. Mei just sat in her stroller and stared.

"Mom, why do you think Mei isn't doing anything?"

"She's probably a little overwhelmed with so much stimulation, Shelly."

"Stimulation?" I asked.

"Yeah, being outdoors, seeing the pandas, the trees, hearing the wind, being with strange people...all of that can be a lot for a baby who's not used to it."

"She doesn't look sad," I said.

"No, but she might be a little confused," Dad added.

We walked until we came to a small building that showed a movie on pandas. We went inside and watched the show. When the movie ended we went into a gift shop.

"Can I buy a souvenir?"

"What would you like?" Dad asked.

I looked around and saw a red T-shirt that had a picture of a black and white panda on it. "This looks nice. I could wear it to school," I said as I picked the shirt up and held it in front of me.

We rode back into town and stopped at a restaurant for lunch. Inside there were large trees growing with branches spreading out and its leaves growing everywhere. It gave the feeling of being outside.

"Lots of feng shui," I said as I sat down between my parents. Our group, now with the six babies, took up three tables. In the center of the table sat the familiar turntable which was our clue that soon we'd be facing lots of Chinese dishes.

Chapter Thirty
One
So Much Red Tape

"Hurry, Shelly, we have to be on the bus in five minutes," Dad called out to me as I finished up in the bathroom.

This was another important day. We went to this office where my parents signed Chinese adoption papers and put a red thumbprint next to their signature. Mei's foot was also recorded and stamped on the adoption documents. A Chinese passport, orphanage documents, adoption certificate, medical records, and Mei's birth certificate all had to be in order. A whole bunch of money was paid to cover expenses and an orphanage donation was given. Once that was all done, we became Mei's new family.

The following day we made a two hour flight from Chengdu to Guangzhou where the American part of the adoption process would be handled. Once we landed, John went off to find our local guide, Jenny. We claimed our luggage and wheeled it off to the bus waiting for us in the parking area.

"Will we be staying at the famous White Swan Hotel?" Dad asked Jenny. She was from Guangzhou, China, but chose an English name to make it easier for Westerners to remember. We learned that all of our Chinese guides did that.

Jenny said, "Yes, the White Swan is the first choice for most adoption groups. In Guangzhou, we call it the Baby Hotel."

The bus took us to Shamian Island where the White Swan was located.

Mrs. Tolson said, "This looks more like France than China."

Jenny laughed. "Great observation. This area was settled by the British and French. A lot of their influence can be seen all around us."

I looked out the bus window and saw buildings with large arch windows and balconies. Many old trees lined the streets with shrubs filling in between. It wasn't long before we pulled up in front of the White Swan.

"Shelly, could you grab that bag and carry it into the hotel for me? I need to carry Mei. She's sound asleep."

"Sure," I replied. "Wow! Look at this place. Are we staying here?"

"Yes," said Jenny. "Do you like it?"

"It's awesome. Look at the water over there."

"That's the Pearl River," said Dad. "Let's go and take a look inside the hotel." Dad picked up two of our bags and we walked into the spacious lobby. Gardens and fountains filled up the huge space inside.

Mrs. Tolson said, "This place is beautiful! It takes my

breath away. What a peaceful escape from the busy city outside."

"Dad, look at that!" On top of a large rock sat an octagonal Chinese pavilion with a gold top.

Jenny took charge of our luggage and had them delivered to our room. She distributed the keys and told us to rest up because tomorrow would be another busy day.

We went up to the room and Dad said he would be happy to stay with Mei while she slept so Mom and I could check out the mall that was in the basement of our hotel.

"Mom, why do so many people adopting Chinese babies stay here?"

"The American Consulate is next door. That's where we need to go to get our official papers. Plus, the hotel knows what we need so they have baby supplies stocked in the hotel stores. That makes things very convenient for us."

We looked around the mall area and found a place that sold 100 percent silk bags.

"These might be good gifts for people back home, Shelly."

"What are they for?" I asked.

"They'll make wonderful jewelry pouches. They're so colorful and easy to pack." I helped Mom pick out ten of them.

"One thing I would like to do before we leave China is find some jade jewelry for both you and Mei," said Mom. "Would you like that? Jenny said we should wait until we get to Hong Kong and buy it there."

"Is jade the green stone we see a lot?"

"Yes, it can be green. Most people think of jade as being green. But it comes in other colors, too."

"Would it be okay if I bought a jade bracelet with the money I've been saving for the trip?"

"I think that could be arranged," Mom said as she

smiled at me. "We're in Hong Kong for two days before we fly home. We'll look for one there."

The following morning we woke up to cooing noises that came from the crib. "Mei seems like such a happy child," Mom said. "We owe a lot to the family that watched over her all these months. They treated her kindly."

I liked my role as big sister. Mei was such fun. Some of the other babies were always crying, but Mei was a calm baby. We were so lucky.

"What are we doing today?" I asked.

"We have lots of red tape to take care of. Legal things we need to do in order to bring Mei into the United States."

John helped all the families fill out the paperwork that was needed. Each of us had a ten minute appointment with the American Consulate. Our appointment was at 3:15 and Mei needed to get a physical exam and have her picture taken before we went. So there was no free time.

At the consulate, we met two women who checked the paperwork. Then my parents went over to a desk to talk to some lady.

"What's that paper?" I asked my parents when they came back out to the waiting room.

"It's an immigrant visa," said Dad as he put it inside an envelope. "This lets Mei leave China and enter into the United States." Everyone was relieved that everything went as planned for all six babies.

"Time for dinner," announced Mr. Knapp. "I found a fried chicken place not too far from the hotel. You guys game for some southern fried chicken?"

"Yes!" I yelled in such a loud voice that people walking by stared at me. I was so embarrassed.

Chapter Thirty Two
Hong Kong

Our group decided to spend two days in Hong Kong before flying home. "As long as we're here, we might as well see it," said Dad.

John was still with us but we had a new local guide. Her name was Lynne, another name changed to sound more English. We arrived at our hotel which was in a great location. It was right in the middle of everything with a subway entrance right across the street.

Hong Kong was much easier to get around. Everything was written in English as well as Chinese. John told us that Hong Kong was once under British rule. So many people spoke English and were more familiar with our Western ways.

After everyone settled in, Lynne took us on a walking

tour around the hotel to see where everything was. She pointed out different restaurants, the post office, and a Chinese laundry. She even took us inside the subway station to explain how to use it.

"On the large map you press your destination." Lynne demonstrated this and the map lit up showing which line to take and how much we'd have to pay for the ticket. "Simply insert your money and a ticket will come out. See? Not hard at all."

"I think we can do that," Dad said to Mom.

"Let's use the subway to go to this place I heard about. It's called Stanley's Market. It's close to the water and there are many stalls set up by the local people selling all kinds of things."

Lynne overheard their conversation and said, "There's a city tour planned for tomorrow morning, and then you'll be on your own for the next day and a half. That would be a good time to go to Stanley Market."

Our city tour proved to be fun. We went to this one place called Ladder Street. Here there were a series of several outdoor escalators leading from one to the next. We used these escalators to get from the street on top of the hill to the streets that were below.

"This is the world's longest covered outdoor escalator," Lynne told us. "It takes about twenty minutes to travel from beginning to end." Each level emptied out onto a street with shops. When we reached the lowest level, everyone scampered off in different directions looking for souvenirs.

After some free time, we met on the bus and rode to a jewelry factory. We had a short demonstration of how they make jewelry followed by a visit to the factory gift shop. That is where we picked out a beautiful jade bracelet for me and a chain with a jade pendent for Mei.

"This will be given to Mei when she's your age,

Shelly," Mom said as she put both small packages into her purse.

Once everyone was back on the bus, we were off to an Aberdeen fishing village. Here we rode on a motorized sampan which was so much fun.

"What kind of boats are those?" I asked pointing across the river to boats that had laundry hanging off the open air deck.

"Those are houseboats that people live on," Dad told me.

"They live on those all the time?"

"Ah huh, the boat is their home," Dad explained.

"Cool, I need to take a picture of that to show Amy."

After a morning of sightseeing, it was time to return to the hotel so all the babies could take a nap.

Mom said, "If these kids don't need a nap, the grownups do. Sightseeing with toddlers is not the easiest thing to do. I forgot what it was like having a wiggly child!"

While Mei and Mom were resting, Dad and I went to the 39th floor of the hotel. A fitness gym was located there plus the most beautiful view of Hong Kong. We were up so high we could see rooftops of smaller buildings near us. Some people had the usual laundry hanging out of their windows. We became used to seeing that. When I looked straight down I saw a man hauling large packages in a small wagon that was towed by an old bicycle. People were everywhere, and where you didn't see a person, you saw a car.

"Shelly, look over there by the concrete steps that go up to the next street. There's a group of kids in green uniforms. I bet they're coming home from school."

"Yeah, they look like they might be my age. I wonder where they live." I watched them until they disappeared into the subway station. "Do they ride the subway all by themselves?" I asked.

"Things are different with kids raised in a large city," Dad answered. "They grow up learning how to take public transportation and become street smart at a young age."

"Dad, we should tell the others about this room at the top of the hotel."

"Good idea. You know what? We leave for home tomorrow morning. We'll come up here tonight to see Hong Kong when it's all lit up."

Chapter Thirty Three
Journey's End

There they are!" cried out Grandma. We got off the airplane to see my grandparents, Aunt Carol, Uncle Charlie, Stephanie, and our entire adoption support group waiting for us. They were holding pink balloons and several signs that said, "Welcome Home". Everyone cheered and eagerly waited to catch their first glimpse of Mei.

"I loved China," I told Stephanie.

"What was it like?"

"We saw pandas, temples, people working in rice paddies, rickshaws attached to bicycles, plus rows and rows of tall buildings with laundry hanging out of the windows drying on poles."

"You had yourself quite an experience," Aunt Carol

said. "Not many kids your age get a chance to go to China."

"Did you learn a lot?" Grandpa asked.

"I did. China is much more to me than a spot on the other side of the globe. It now has a face."

Just then we heard Mei crying. Besides our little group, the other families that traveled to China all had people waiting for them, too. We filled up the room. All this confusion frightened Mei. Mom comforted her and told her it was okay. Grandma smiled and kept repeating how beautiful she was.

After our homecoming, my grandparents drove us to our house. It was seven o'clock at night and after twenty-four hours of traveling, we were tired.

Grandma said, "We'll drop you off so you can rest. Then we'll stop by to see you tomorrow."

"Do I have to go to school tomorrow?" I asked Mom.

"Tomorrow is Sunday, Shelly. No school on Sunday."

"Sunday? I said. "It's weird how I lost track of what day of the week it was."

"That's partly because you weren't doing your regularly scheduled activities," Mom explained.

"Plus don't forget jetlag," Grandma added.

"I'm glad I don't have to go to school tomorrow."

It was funny seeing our house after being gone for two weeks. I felt like I wasn't really in it.

"Why does our house look the same but seem larger to me?" I asked.

"That's because you've been living in hotel rooms," Dad explained.

"Let's show Mei her purple room," Mom said. Dad picked her up and carried her upstairs.

"Here's your new room, Mei," Dad said. Mei's eyes were quite large as she looked at the painted balloons on the wall. Her head turned in all directions. Mom laid her down on the changing table that was set up next to the dresser and started taking her clothes off.

"Want me to get her pajamas out of the dresser?" I asked.

"Would you?" Mom brought her into the bathroom and put a little water in the tub. Mei started crying just like she did when she was taking a bath in China.

"Mei, it's okay," I said as I rubbed her arm. "You'll get used to this. There's so much for all of us to get used to."

When the bath was over, Mei stopped crying and Mom dressed her in the new pj's.

"Shelly, how about giving Mei her bottle?" Mom asked.

I quickly sat in the chair and Mom put Mei in my lap with a pillow under her head. She eagerly grabbed at the bottle and started drinking the milk. I looked down at her and both of us stared into each other's eyes. Mei gulped down the milk, stopped for a few seconds with the bottle tightly clutched in her mouth, and gave a loud sigh. All during this time she never stopped looking at me. She continued drinking the milk until I saw her heavy eyes begin to close. She opened them until they could no longer stay open.

"Mom," I whispered. "Mei's sleeping." Mom came into the room, picked her up, and placed her in the crib. We stood there a few minutes and watched her sleep as she breathed in and out.

"So what do you think, Shelly?"

"I never knew how neat it would be having a little sister."

Mom hugged me, turned off the light, and said, "I'm so glad. Let's get some sleep ourselves. It's been a long journey."

Mom walked out of the room and I started to follow.

But something made me stop and look back at the crib that no longer was empty.

"Yes," I whispered under my breath. "It has been a long journey—this journey to Mei."

Canals of Suzhou

The Great Wall of China

Hong Kong

Hong Kong Waterfront

Panda Sanctuary in Chengdu

Shanghai

Terraced rice paddies

TerracottaWarriors of Xi'an

Tiananmen Square in Beijing

Printed in the United States
93977LV00005B/160/A